VICTORIA'S PARK

VICTORIA'S PARK

A Very Sweet Revenge!

Barrie S. Haynes

B.J. HAYNES

Matador
5 Weir Road
Kibworth Beauchamp
Leicester LE8 0LQ, UK
Tel: (+44) 116 279 2299
Fax: (+44) 116 279 2277
Email: books@troubador.co.uk
Web: www.troubador.co.uk/matador

ISBN 978 1848765 511

British Library Cataloguing in Publication Data.
A catalogue record for this book is available from the British Library.

Typeset in 10.5pt Palatino by Troubador Publishing Ltd, Leicester, UK

Matador is an imprint of Troubador Publishing Ltd

Printed in Great Britain by the MPG Books Group, Bodmin and King's Lynn

To Christopher
who left us too soon

"There is no such thing as a fresh flame. A flame has no substance it springs from nowhere and dies to nothing. It rearranges the fabric which returns with an improved similitude.

Edwin Baker.
'The Cleansing Flame'
(pub. 1752)

CHAPTER ONE

"FIRE!"

"I want to go home! I want to go home now! Vicki could not remember the last time she had raised her voice she was normally more of a mouse than a lion. It did feel good however, so once more she roared out, "I want to go home, I want to go home!" A young nurse came running into the cubical, drew the curtain shut and whispered, "Please Mrs. Smith, please keep your voice down, the whole of A & E can hear you. We have some very sick people out there."

"I don't care," said Vicki, "I've had enough. Do you know that I could have been killed?"

"Yes I know," replied the nurse. "But we have to wait for the doctor to give the ok, he will be back in a few minutes when he's sorted out a lady from St. Martin's Drive, who had a panic attack when she heard the explosion."

"Heard the explosion?" cried Vicki "I caused the explosion! I was there, I could have lost my face!"

"Well you haven't," said the nurse, "You have only lost your eyebrows, and Dr. Snell says that they will grow back, eventually."

"Eventually?" screamed Vicki. "How long is eventually?"

"About a year," replied the nurse, who had no idea of the timescale.

"And what about my hair, how long is that going to take?"

1

"You haven't lost your hair," said the nurse, who was now peeping through a gap in the curtain, looking in vain for the doctor.

After a long pause she added "It's just a bit frizzy at the front, if the colour doesn't come back you can always give it a bit of a tint."

At this point, Vicki was toying with the idea of inflicting serious bodily harm on the nurse, who after all, would not have to go far for treatment.

A voice called, "Mandy are you there? Can you go to the ambulance station? RTA coming in." Mandy took off, vanishing into a sea of white coats and bandages. Someone passing the cubicle shut the curtain.

"Do I look that bad?" shouted Vicki, staring at the huge light over her bed.

As Vicki waited for the doctor she reflected on the morning's events. She may have lost her eyebrows, but she had not lost her memory. There was also a strange feeling that this could be a new beginning, a new start with a new face. What had really happened up at the Bowls Club? Whatever the cause, she knew deep down that it was not her fault, and somewhere, in a recess at the back of her mind, there was a nagging suspicion that Peter had a hand in it.

It had been her first visit to the new Liddingdale Bowls Club, built on an old sandpit at a place called Abbey Wood. This had been a huge rubbish dump for many years, before being covered with a thin layer of earth. Vicki's neighbour, Doris, had asked her to go and make refreshments for the bowlers, who might be having a game up there. She told her it would not be busy on a Monday morning, and when

Vicki arrived at the Club, she found only two members present, Joe Willmott, a short, dapper little chap, and Charlie Simms, large and clumsy, a boxer in his youth with the nose to prove it. Both were retired, and members of the Town Council. Vicki's husband had been the Mayor of Liddingdale for the last four years. The reason Peter was still the Mayor was that nobody else wanted the job.

If the town was forced to introduce a new 'device' to replace the present one (an effeminate looking monk sat on a wooden throne) it would take the form of the back of someone's head with the slogan 'APATHY' inscribed below.

At eleven o clock precisely, Vicki decided to boil the kettle. She found a box of matches in the kitchen of the small pavilion, and went to light one of the gas rings on a second hand cooker that stood in the corner. She turned on the gas and lit the match. Things happened very fast. First a huge flame rose up in front of her face, then, a loud bang threw her on the floor. The latter probably saved Vicki from a visit to the plastic surgeon. She looked up and saw that the whole building was on fire. A big hand grabbed her and dragged her out onto the green. She looked up into Charlie's eyes and said "Wow! What the?" but was cut short as Charlie picked her up, and along with Joe, ran to the edge of the green to get away from the heat. From here they could see the pavilion engulfed in flames. Joe called the Fire Brigade on his mobile, and then insisted that he call an ambulance for Vicki, who was now shouting "My car, my car!" which had been parked around the back of the building. A loud explosion told them that her car, an old Astra that Peter had bought for her from one of his friends in the scrap metal business, was no more.

"I knew this would happen," said Joe.

"Aye," said Charlie, a man of few words.

"They should never have built on this land," said Joe. "It's the gas, look, it's more than the club house that's on fire, there are flames coming up all over the place. Where the hell is the fire engine? All that second hand timber came from Benson's when they pulled it down, been at the scrap yard for years in the big shed. No wonder it went up like a roman candle, it was as dry as a bone!"

"Aye," said Charlie, holding Vicki a little tighter than was really necessary.

"What was wrong with the old green?" asked Joe, "Why did we have to move?"

"Regeneration," answered Vicki, regaining her composure and pulling away from Charlie, but not sure if she could stand on her own.

"Regeneration my backside!" said Joe, "It's your husband, he wants to put a great big ugly supermarket down there, right by the river! It were a lovely site. On a slow day we used to feed the swans between ends. In summer, we had tea on the veranda in proper cups!"

"Aye," said Charlie.

A distant siren heralded the arrival of the town's best fire engine, followed closely by Tom, the Fire Chief. By the time they arrived, the pavilion was a blackened heap of charcoal on the edge of a black rectangle that for seven days had been a bowling green. The fire crew went through the motions and put on a fine display, but alas the new Liddingdale Bowling Club was a total loss. While the firefighters rushed around playing with their hoses, the Chief walked slowly over to Vicki and said in a low voice,

"I knew this would happen. I told Peter, I knew this would happen, sooner or later, I knew this would happen!"

"So did I," said Joe, not wanting to be left out, "It's the gas. Methane given off by the waste, old nappies, uneaten food, decaying chemicals. God knows what's down there!"

"Aye," said Charlie.

"Oh yes!" said the Chief, "They were warned, the whole lot of them, especially Mr.Smith!"

"And some of us protested, but were out-voted," shouted Joe, trying to contain his temper and remembering that Mrs Smith, who he rather fancied, was standing beside him and had just been blown up.

Vicki wanted to say something, anything in favour of her husband, but the words didn't come.

At this point the ambulance arrived. A young girl, who was driving, jumped out and put a large blanket around Vicki, then helped her into the back.

"How do I look?" asked Vicki.

"You'll be fine," the girl replied, "You'll be just fine."

"Hello there," said the doctor as he threw back the curtain.

"Can I go home now?" pleaded Vicki.

"I think so," said the doctor, who had a kind face and a pleasant manner. "You've had a bad shock, so don't drive."

"No chance of that!" replied Vicki, "The car's gone with the club house along with my handbag, I will have to phone my husband, has he been informed?"

"We called him," said the doctor, "But when we told him it was not life threatening and that we would probably

5

release you later today, he said that he would be home around five."

Vicki stared at the doctor in disbelief and replied, "He'll have to drive me home."

"That would be wise," the doctor replied, "We will give you some tablets to relieve the pain and help you sleep. We'll need to see you in a few days, I will make an appointment. We need to assess the situation you may want some sort of cosmetic surgery and perhaps counselling. I must warn you that your face might never be quite what it was, on the other hand, you still have your sight and the damage is only skin deep as far as we can tell, now is there anything else that you require?"

"Yes," said Vicki.

"A mirror."

CHAPTER TWO

REGENERATION

St. Mary's is a town church, solid and foursquare. It looks as if it has been made out of toy building blocks. Dominating the centre of Liddingdale, it is big and ungainly with no pretensions to grandeur. Inside, a hotchpotch of dark corners and over elaborate columns lead you into the barn-like nave, lit from the west by a huge window. People come from far and wide to view this marvel of Victorian optimism. If you climb to the top of the sturdy tower, a good view of the town and surrounding area may be obtained.

The town spreads out below and if you look carefully, you may just make out the ragged pattern of a medieval street plan. Liddingdale is a mixture of styles, there is an exceptionally ugly town hall, completed in 1887 just in time for the Queen's jubilee. Its one redeeming feature is the ornate campanile, a perfect foil to the plain church tower on the opposite side of the Market Place. If you look a little beyond the town hall you will see a small open space, known optimistically as 'The Park'. This is the site of the great 'Abbey of the Dales' now reduced to a couple of broken arches covered in ivy.

Looking away from the centre, the rest is urban sprawl of the worst kind. Although the town came through World War Two unscathed, it did not escape the brutal concrete of a later age.

The town centre is built of local sandstone, mixed here

7

and there with mellow brick. The rest is a muddy puddle of cheap houses, car lots and factory outlets. Walking around the tower you will see that there is only one main road running north to south.

Liddingdale is an ancient place. The road that cuts through the centre is still known as 'The Drove' and is the reason for the town's existence, for this was the cattle road for over two thousand years. Here, the drovers crossed the River Lid by a shallow ford later replaced by the Town Bridge in the 16th cent. A great abbey was established under the Normans and the town flourished until the dissolution. After a period of decline, new industry came in the 18th cent when it was discovered that the sand, upon which the town stands, had properties that led to the manufacture of high quality glass. A large factory sprung up and brought great prosperity for two hundred years until the industry declined in the 1960s. With its heart ripped out, Liddingdale fell asleep.

Most people who work now commute to Leeds and Manchester via the M62 corridor, while many of the young (esp. the brighter ones) have forsaken their home for pastures new and a future.

Now that you have become accustomed to the view, you will see new bits in the pattern. You will see scars dotted around the edges, these are the sandpits. More than twenty could once be seen but nature is starting to reclaim them. One of the largest is the home of 'Smith's Recycling' established by a local man, George Smith, in 1953. This enterprise is now run by his son, Vicki's husband and Mayor of Liddingdale. The largest of all the sandpits was at a place called Abbey Wood.

8

You will see it out on the higher ground to the west, a large bumpy area devoid of trees and grass. It looks like an abandoned battlefield on some remote planet where life is in its infancy. We are looking at a large landfill site that took over twenty years to fill.

The Town Council, under Peter Smith, want to develop the site. There are plans to build a sports complex and theme park and these are in the town hall and inside Peter Smith's head, all filed under that horrible buzz-word much loved by councillors and politicians.

REGENERATION!

CHAPTER THREE

"RHUBARB!"

Vicki Smith took a deep breath and looked down at the small mirror that Dr. Snell had given her. It was the same face as before, the only difference was the colour and the hair. Her once fair skin was now a series of red patches, each patch a slightly different hue. In between there were dark streaks and islands of brown, the shade you would get if you left the sun lamp on too long. As she had a round face, the whole ensemble reminded her of a rhubarb crumble in its bowl. The hair was another matter, most of it looked the same except for the bit at the very front which stuck out, looking like the branch of an old tree that had been hit by a cattle truck in a narrow lane. For some reason she was not too bothered about her new look.

Vicki marched through the ward, making for reception. As she weaved between the beds, chairs and trolleys, she noticed one or two stares from people, but shrugged this off as normal behaviour for those not used to rhubarb crumble. At the desk she asked to use the telephone. The Receptionist, who had the face of a vulture, and an ugly one at that, asked if she had authority. "Dr. Snell said it would be alright," replied Vicki in a rasping voice that she had not heard before. The Receptionist, fumbled under her desk and brought out a telephone.

"Nine for an outside line," she barked, then vanished

behind a huge monitor and started to abuse an innocent looking keyboard.

Vicki picked up the handset and punched out Peter's work's number. After a while the phone was answered by Dave, the foreman.

"Is Peter there?" she asked.

"No, sorry, he's had to go out, Council Business. Is that you Mrs. S, are you alright? I heard what happened, terrible! Is there anything I can do?"

"It's ok Dave, if he comes back this afternoon, just ask him to come home ASAP," replied Vicki.

She then called Peter's mobile, but just got the usual message.

A little downcast, she replaced the receiver and shouted "Thank you so very much!" to the ugly Receptionist. Vicki made for the doors and walked out into the sunshine. A woman coming into the hospital gave her a stare. Vicki looked her in the eye and said "Rhubarb!"

In the car park, she decided to walk the two miles to her home on the edge of town. It was a beautiful afternoon, and after all the excitement, she was glad to be alive. Three or four people in the Market Place rubbernecked, and to each one she gave a polite "Rhubarb!"

On arriving home, she realised that she did not have a key. Close to tears, she sat down on the front door step and pondered her immediate future.

17 Abbeyfield Drive is a large detached house in the "Tudor Style" of the 1930s. It has a stained glass sailing boat on the front door with leaded diamond glass in the rest of the windows, the lead now stuck on, thanks to double glazing. Number seventeen was not good enough

for Ascot, but it could have held its own in one of the nicer parts of Worthing.

There was no sign of Doris, Vicki did not like Doris very much, Doris was a snob and looked down her nose at everybody in the road except Peter. Doris adored Peter. To have the Mayor living next door was as good as a lottery win. Ladies of a certain age in Liddingdale adored Peter. He was good looking, charming and clever, but he could also be very selfish, and like most men of his kind, he liked having sex, but he didn't really like or understand women. There was only one special "girl" in his life and that wasn't Vicki.

After a few minutes, she realised that she would have to break a window. But which one? She tried to remember if there was a spare key in the garage (which was locked). That seemed the best bet. All she needed now was a hammer. Vicki walked to the potting shed at the end of her long, well tended garden, and found a small ancient hammer in a box of tools under the bench. She realised, when she got back to the garage, that the windows were too high for her to reach. Despondent, she sat down on the back lawn and waited for her husband to return. In a rare fit of temper she threw the hammer across the lawn, aiming it at a rather stupid gnome that Doris had bought her years ago. She scored a direct hit, striking him on his ample waist. He toppled over onto his back, knocking his head off on the bird bath as he went down, the lifeless torso still clinging to a little fishing rod.

At precisely seventeen hundred hours a sleek new Jaguar purred up the driveway, crunching the gravel with its huge truck-like tyres. As Peter got out, he looked back lovingly at the beast, her shiny black body glowing in the late afternoon sun. He opened one of the rear doors and picked up his executive leather briefcase from the back seat, then walked to the front door of the house and let himself in.

From the kitchen window he noticed the dead gnome and Vicki sitting next to it like an undernourished pigeon. He opened one of the windows and shouted, "What the hell are you doing? "You stupid cow!"

"What does it look like Pratface?" replied Vicki, "I've been waiting for you all afternoon!"

Peter, who had never been called Pratface before, was temporarily lost for words.

"I didn't have a key, I lost my handbag in the fire," continued Vicki, with an inner strength that she had never felt before, "And by the way, the car's gone and Tom wants to see you down at the Fire Station about that dodgy landfill!"

By this time Peter was out in the garden with his hands stretched out in front of him, ready to throttle his wife. Vicki stood up and faced him. She saw the look of disbelief in his cold eyes, and was just about to shout Rhubarb! when he said, "Your face, it's red! Can't you do something?"

"I might be able to soften it a little if I could get into the house," she replied, "But I'm afraid the doctor said that only time will heal the scars. But don't worry, I'll stay away from all Council meetings and social events."

Peter turned away. As he made for the kitchen, he said quietly,

"Well that's alright then."

Dinner passed in silence, Vicki suggested that they had a "takeaway", but her husband demanded that she cook him something. Peter was an only child, and his mother had doted on him, he wanted for nothing, he had every toy in the shop.

His father was a gentleman in the broadest sense, who had built up a business from nothing.

When he died at the early age of fifty, Peter took on a very healthy bank balance which he had been spending ever since. "Smith's Re cycling" was in a bad way. Not many people in the town knew, although some, like Tom, Joe and Charlie had their suspicions. Peter was selfish and self - centred. He had been a reasonable dad to their son Jamie, who was now married and living in Altrincham. Jamie did not like his father very much, and after leaving university, he had moved away and was now a Project Manager for 'North West Castings'. He once told his father, he didn't want to be a Rag and Bone Man! Perhaps Peter's most endearing quality was that he was not at all fussy about his grub. He would eat anything, and because of the way that he shovelled it down, he probably didn't taste it anyway.

After a simple meal of ham, egg and chips, Peter sat down in his armchair and fell asleep in front of the television. He did this most evenings, but this evening was different, Vicki wanted to talk. 'Far North Television' and the local BBC station had mentioned the fire briefly, both stating that it may have been caused by a faulty cooker. "Are you worried about the publicity?" asked Vicki waking Peter up with a start.

"I have nothing to fear, that cooker was checked over thoroughly by an expert," he replied.

"Where did it come from?" asked Vicki.

"Through the trade," said Peter, before he nodded off again.

An hour later Vickie woke him up again, she was standing over him when she asked,

"Methane gas, is it dangerous?"

"There's no methane up there," he replied, "I've had the whole area thoroughly checked over, there's no methane or any other gas up there, except for the bottle of gas for the stove, that you destroyed along with everything else this morning!"

Vicki suddenly felt very old, the events of the day had taken their toll, and she went to bed, only to be woken up later by her husband, who had also decided to have an 'early night'.

Vicki had been a good and faithful wife, but in recent times it was her home, garden and son that took up most of her affection. As she lay there next to a grunting shape that was once Liddingdale's answer to Elvis, she thought perhaps life may have been different if she had married Cyril Parker, the Undertaker's son. Vicki wanted to talk and for some reason she blurted out "Do you know in two weeks time I will be fifty?"

"It's no big deal love," replied Peter in that disjointed speech people have when they are half asleep, "I've been fifty for two years now!"

"Jamie called the other day, said he might come over." said Vicki, now talking very loud to keep Peter awake.

"Come over for what?" asked Peter.

"For my birthday party of course!" replied Vicki.

"And who says you're having one?" he asked "What's

15

so special about fifty?"

"If you can afford a new Jag, you can take me away for my birthday," she said brightly.

"And just where would her ladyship like to go?" he asked in a sarcastic tone.

"New York" replied Vicki, "I think I'd like to go to New York."

CHAPTER FOUR

"NIGHT SHIFT"

Vicki turned over and quickly went off to sleep dreaming of carriage rides in Central Park, the sun streaming onto Grand Central concourse, walking down Forty Second Street, eating a bagel with a shmeer. Peter lay there wondering what exactly had happened to his wife in the explosion. As he thought about what to do next the bedside telephone rang.

"Hello," said Peter. "Yes, yes, ok I understand, hold up on the A1, long diversion, ok, give me twenty minutes and put all your lights out, we don't want to attract the local plod."

Peter dressed, grabbed his keys, and within ten minutes was making his way across town to the scrapyard. A delivery had arrived late, very late indeed. Peter did not drive through the town centre, which would have been the quickest route. He took the by-roads and lanes, and these included Monk Lane, where he passed the site of the Bowling Club. He noticed that the police had cordoned it off with that fancy tape they use. I wonder how long they took to turn up, he mused as the big black car effortlessly cut through the dark. On arriving at the yard he saw a large lorry in front of the gates. The driver must have been looking in his mirror, for as soon as Peter stopped, the guy was out of his cab and running toward him.

"Sorry about this," he said, "But I've got to offload this tonight. Strict instructions from the Boss."

"What is it?" Peter enquired.

"Don't know," said the Driver "But I don't think it's very nice. You need to keep it out of sight."

Peter unlocked the heavy gates to let the lorry draw in. He then followed in the Jaguar and relocked the gates. The driver pulled back the side curtain on the trailer to reveal, in the poor light, a full load of large black oil drums.

"I'll get the fork lift," said Peter.

"For God's sake be careful," said the Driver, taking a pack of cigarettes out of his coat pocket.

"Leave this to me," Peter whispered, "Go and have a smoke and come back in half an hour."

Peter gave the driver the keys to the office, where the guy could make a cup of tea, and got on with the job in hand. Peter was no stranger to fork lifts, (he drove his first one at the age of five on his father's knee) and soon had the drums stashed away at the back of the yard. Tomorrow a pile of old cars would be dumped in front of them. As the lorry left the yard the driver handed Peter a fat brown envelope. "It's all there," he said. Peter got into his car. As the clock on the dashboard turned to twelve he picked up his phone and called Angela Sadler.

"Hi," said Angela brightly, as if she had just come off a customer care course in some dreary motorway hotel, "Where the hell have you been Peter? I've missed you."

"Business Angela, business," replied Peter.

"Funny business if I know you!" said Angela in a sarcastic tone. "What do you want? I was just going to bed."

"Can I come over?" asked Peter.

"What for?" asked Angela.

"To talk" said Peter.

"Is that all?" she replied. "Well ok, but be quiet and don't park that great big car outside my house."

Inspector Angela Sadler of the North Moorland Police, lived in a new house on the very edge of town It was near to the scrapyard and it took Peter only a few minutes to get there. He parked his car on a farm track and went to the back door which had been left ajar. Angela met him in the kitchen, they kissed, and then she ushered him into the lounge where they sat together on a large settee. "My, it's been a while," said Angela, "Have you got problems? I heard about Vicki, is she alright?"

"Well no, not really," Peter replied, "She is acting a bit scary. Wants to go to New York for her birthday. I think it might be the shock of what's happened, but I've got bigger problems at the moment. I'm running out of money."

"So what's new?" Angela asked, "You spend it like water."

"I'm worried about this fire," said Peter, "Tom is suspicious and he could stop the scheme for a new sports complex and theme park over at Abbey Wood."

"Don't worry about Tom," replied Angela, "He's got form, way back, in Scotland, all hushed up at the time. He's also been a very naughty boy recently. I turned a blind eye, so he owes me a favour."

"But it's not just Tom, it's the money. We, well I, was hoping to get some more from the Regeneration Fund. I've a guy from the EU coming here in the Autumn, do you know anybody high up who needs a favour? This scheme could create five hundred jobs!"

"Fifty crap jobs more like!" snorted Angela.

"I don't see that," said Peter, sounding a bit upset.

19

"You don't see a lot of things! Shall we go upstairs?"

"What for?"

"Cops and robbers?"

"I don't know, it's been a long day."

"I've brought a spare uniform from the Station."

"Alright then."

When Peter arrived back in Abbeyfield Drive the dawn was breaking. He entered the house on tip-toe. Vicki was fast asleep. At breakfast she was annoyingly cheerful and kept patting him on the head. If this was not bad enough she kept singing, "I love New York in June" over and over. She cooked him his favourite breakfast, a huge fry up with extra black pudding, and put seven spoonfuls of sugar in his tea. She then watched him intently as he struggled to eat it.

"ALLRIGHT!" he suddenly blurted out, "ALLRIGHT YOU CAN GO! BUT NOT FOR YOUR BIRTHDAY, I'LL PLAN SOMETHING ELSE, SOMETHING THAT'S NICE, WE'LL GO TO NEW YORK IN THE AUTUMN WHEN I HAVE MORE TIME!"

"In the fall dear," she said sweetly, "In the Fall dear. That's what the Americans call it, the Fall."

Vicki patted him on the head once more and went off down the garden to repair the gnome. Peter went to the bathroom and threw up.

CHAPTER FIVE

"A WHITER SHADE OF GREY"

Bill Barnswold took the slip road off the motorway, crossed the bridge, and took the old drover's road towards Liddingdale. It had been years since his last visit, but once he had known the area well. That was in the days when 'Bensons' the glass makers were the main employer in town and their wares were being exported all over the world. Bill was in the Army in those days, having joined up straight from school. Within five years he had been made Corporal and had seen service abroad in one or two "Hot Spots:" He was a modest man and never talked or boasted about where he had been or what he had done. While in the north of England on a training course, he had met his wife, Mary. She had been born and brought up in Liddingdale. Soon after they were married, Bill left the Army and took her to Sheffield where he had grown up.

Bill had just retired and was thinking of moving to Spain, when out of the blue he received a call from a friend of his mother- in law telling him that she had died at the age of ninety six. She was a lovely lady and was always very fond of Bill, as she had six daughters but no sons. Mary had died young and as the years passed Bill's visits to the town became few and far between, but he never lost touch completely, and now he was on his way to attend her funeral. He also had a call from her solicitor asking him to pop round when convenient, to discuss her will.

21

As Bill approached the town, he saw ahead the outline of St. Mary's riding on the sky behind the out-of-town carpet stores and dreary estates of executive housing, full of cars and tiny gardens. The sight of St. Mary's, where he was married, reminded him of his Mary. Why did she have to die so young? Why do so many good people die young? He had asked a priest once, but the answer he received was far from satisfactory. One morning she did not wake up, and that was that. He never really knew why, nobody did, she just died, "Her heart," they said, it just stopped beating.

He was brought back to the present by a red traffic light on the south side of the town bridge. At least that's not changed, he thought. They were going to widen the bridge years ago, when Mary was a lass. They were going to widen the bridge when her mother, Enid was a lass. He drove across the bridge and then turned into the Market Place. At the far end he drove under the arch and into the small car park of the Engineers Arms Hotel, his home for the next few days. After checking in, he decided to go for a walk round the town centre, and if possible, get a haircut before the funeral on the following day. The first thing he noticed was that the town seemed to be sleeping. Many of the shops were closed down and a couple of pubs were missing altogether. One thing that surprised him was although the place was drab, some of the buildings had been cleaned up. Now that the glass works had gone they would never get that dirty again. The big church and town hall looked "well scrubbed". But dirt sticks, it gets under the skin, into the very soul, and on closer inspection, the town had not shaken off it's industrial past. It was not grey anymore, but it was not completely clean either. It was just a whiter shade of grey.

In a small gift shop by the church he asked the lady serving if there was a barber's shop nearby, to which she replied that they had all closed down over the years, but he could go "unisex".

"I haven't tried that yet," laughed Bill.

"You should," said the lady, who had taken a bit of a shine to him, 'The Bella Vista Hair and Beauty Salon' is the place to go. It's very nice there, fix you up like Marlon Brando!"

"He's dead," replied Bill.

The "Bella Vista" was just around the corner in Duke Street. It was larger than Bill had expected, taking up what had been at one time three shops. Pushing gently on the door he entered the unknown world of unisex. A dozen pairs of female eyes stared back at him from the dark and mysterious interior. A good electrician could fix this, he thought, as a large woman approached.

"Hello young man!" she said in a deep, rather satisfying voice, "And what can we do for you today, a trim round or the full works?"

"What's the full works?" asked Bill as more eyes came out of the gloom.

"About fifty quid," she replied.

"I'll have a trim round," said Bill wishing he was back in Sheffield.

She ushered him into a side room and switched on the light which was much brighter than he had expected. She sat him in an enormous leather chair and whispered, "Back in a jiffy."

Left to his own devices, Bill took in his surroundings. Apart from the ceiling, the whole room was black, the walls relieved by huge pictures of semi-naked young men. Each one had a different hairstyle. The nearest to Bill's requirements was the "Young Dude" which he thought he might ask for. What would his father think if he was alive? What would his mates in Sheffield say if they knew he was going unisex for the first time?

After a few minutes she came back, carrying an old fashioned cut throat razor. For a time there was silence as she concentrated on the job in hand. Then she said in her deep rich voice, "Have you been on any holidays this year, or is this your first one?"

"It's not a holiday," said Bill, "Although I love the area, I'm up here for my Mother-in Law's funeral tomorrow."

"Oh I am sorry," she replied, "Comes to us all eventually. Was she a good age?"

"Ninety six," replied Bill, "A lovely lady." As the tears welled up, he told her all about the Army, Mary and Sheffield. There was then a silent period while she tidied him up, and looking pleased with the result she said, "Who's a pretty boy then?"

Bill made to go, searching in his jacket pocket for some money, but she pushed him back into the chair with a force that surprised him.

"My name's Jessie, but everybody calls me Jess. What's yours?"

"Bill," he replied, "Just Bill."

"Look Bill," said Jessie, "I know you will find this hard to believe, but I know things. I think that you need to stay on here after the funeral. I think that there's somebody here in Liddingdale who might need you. Don't ask me how I know, I just know these things."

Taken aback Bill replied, "Look Jessie, sorry, Jess, for the first time in my life I'm free, free as a bird. I'm sure you can understand, I don't want to get involved, I don't want commitment."

Jessie laughed, "Not me, don't be daft, but there is someone, I don't know who, but someone needs your help. Then you can go off to Benidorm and play bingo for the rest of your life. By the way where are you staying?"

"The Engineer's Arms," replied Bill sheepishly.

"I drink there," said Jessie, "Round the back in the Welder's Bar. Come and meet the girls, I'm usually there on a Wednesday night and at weekends."

As he left the Bella Vista Bill asked Jessie where the name came from, wondering if it was a momento of a holiday, long ago. Jessie laughed, "Oh no," she said, "My brother Clive ran a guest house with that name. Pinched it off him."

"Sounds exotic," said Bill "Where was it?"

"In Bognor Regis," said Jessie, "I met the Captain there. He was my second husband, lovely man, twenty years older and with only one leg, lost the other one in 1942."

"Where was that?" asked Bill.

"Southampton," she replied. "Going down to the Solent, no lights for navigation complete blackout."

"Yes," said Bill gravely, "They must have been dangerous times. "Was it enemy fire or a mine?"

"Nothing like that," Jessie replied,

"Run over by a tram."

CHAPTER SIX

"BEFORE THE STORM"

The two weeks leading up to Vicki's birthday was a quiet time in Liddingdale. The weather was perfect for early summer, not too hot with a gentle breeze and clear blue skies. Vicki was looking forward to her birthday. She had spring cleaned the house and garden from top to bottom and even bought a brand new gnome (without fishing rod), as a companion to the one that had been hit by the hammer. Peter had reluctantly provided her with another car, an Aspandino (all spare parts, no din number) which, although much older that the Astra, suited her better as there was more room in the back for the shopping. To Vicki, a car was transportation at its crudest level. During this time, she made a couple of visits to the hospital, where her face was assessed. The opinion of the doctors was that it would heal naturally, but there might be scars. Vicki would have to wait until nature had taken its course, after which she could, if she wished, take further action. For some reason, Vicki was not at all bothered.

She started to make numerous journeys into town to buy guide books and DVD's about North America, and New York in particular. In the evenings she would talk non stop to Peter about the 'Big Apple', although for much of the time during this period he was away from home. The 'rhubarb crumble' was becoming more 'stewed peaches with custard' as the days passed, and although there was no sign of an eyebrow on the horizon, Jessie down at the Bella Vista had fixed her up with a very convincing pencil, so that she could have a different one every day.

The only little cloud to dampen her mood was that Jamie couldn't make it for the big day, as he had to go on a 'Group Training Weekend', where he would help to build a rope bridge across a non existent river, near Scunthorpe.

Most of the land around Liddingdale was owned by the 'Liddingbury Estate', whose rights went as far back as the Norman Conquest. When the Abbey had closed they were given more land nearer to the town. Later they grabbed much of the Common Land used by the townspeople and the drovers. The site at Abbey Wood, including the whole of the landfill belonged to the town, being purchased in 1802 from the then Lord Liddingbury after he had made a great loss at the gaming tables. The Corporation of Liddingdale had leased the land for two hundred years to industry and for the excavation of sand. After the factory's demise, the land had come back into Corporation hands.

The Council, under Peter's guidance, had already obtained a grant of half a million pounds for regeneration of the site, but a lot of this had been swallowed up on jollies abroad or 'fact finding missions' as they are known. There had also been trips to other northern towns involving the whole council, the Mayor's Rolls Royce and on one occasion, a helicopter. Peter was confident that he could get more funds from the Government and the EU in the future but he still needed private investment, and to this end he spent a 'Fact Finding Weekend' in a Wemyss Bay Hotel with June Thompson, Chief Executive of

'Thompson's Super Savers Stores'. To allay suspicion, he went by train, and even got Vicki to drive him to the station. June was quite willing to contribute to the new 'Abbey Wood Centre & Theme Park' if she could build a "Thompson's Megastore" on the old Bowling Club site by the town bridge, just outside the conservation area.

Peter invited June to come and meet the Council on the 20th, which was Vicki's birthday.

Bill Barnswold had stayed on in Liddingdale after the funeral. The following day he had made a visit to the solicitor where to his surprise he found out that Enid had left him her tiny bungalow in Mill Street. To him this gift was bittersweet, as Enid had outlived all of her children. She had been careful with her brass, as they say in those parts, and had seen her grandchildren well provided for, although none had turned up for the funeral. Later that day he walked round to Mill Street and inspected his new asset. It was old, it smelled old and it looked old. Inside everything was old. He sat in the small kitchen and decided to clean the place up and put it on the market for whatever it might fetch. He had a house in Stannington which he wanted to sell, but for now, he would put that on the back burner. Another reason to stay was Jessie. It was not passion, not even physical, he just liked her, she made him laugh, just like Mary had done all those years ago. He kept thinking of the Bella Vista and remembering when he was a lad, the Barber would ask, "Anything for the weekend Sir?" He started to think that he would like Jessie for the weekend.

On Saturday night he summoned up the courage to visit the "Welder's Bar" round the back of the hotel. As he entered he saw Jessie at the bar with half a dozen big women. Around the room were more women of all ages and shapes.

"Don't be shy," shouted a lady wearing a tent.

"You leave him alone!" cried Jess, "This is our Bill, come over here love, let me get you a drink."

Jess read the startled look on Bill's face and said gently, "Don't worry we're not all lesbians, we just come here to get away from men and have a laugh now and then. Besides you're not the only man here, there's little Allan hiding over there in the corner, and he's gay."

"I am not," protested Allan, "I thought he were a lady!"

"Nasty business," said Jessie, "Hasn't been anywhere near Halifax since that night."

CHAPTER SEVEN

"HAPPY BIRTHDAY"

On the morning of June 20th Vicki had a lie in as she wanted to be bright and bouncy for the evening's festivities. When she did emerge, she found that Peter had already left the house. He had mentioned the evening before that he had some council business to attend to, so she was not at all concerned. She had a light breakfast and drove down to Jessie's for a make-over. At the Bella Vista she had her hair styled in a new exciting way with the front, fire damaged bit, chopped off. The result was unique.

Peter, who had forgotten about Vicki's birthday, was busy sorting out the last minute details of the special meeting where June would explain her plans for a megastore, and, more importantly, reveal how much money the town would receive towards the Abbey Wood complex. He had decided to hold the meeting away from prying eyes at the "Sky Mountain Resort" out on the High Dale Road. This was really an old hunting lodge that had been enlarged. The dry ski slope at the side had long ago become a weed strewn track.

Peter's pride and joy was a scale model of the Abbey Wood development, perfect in every detail. It had cost the Council Tax Payer £2500 which he thought was great value for money, as he considered it a magnet for attracting private sector money to the scheme. Looking down on the model, the sports complex looked like a big letter 'H' with a large swimming pool on one side and a "Multi Sports Amenity Building" opposite, this latter facility rising to four storeys, with a great number of indoor playing areas.

Joining the two together was a huge indoor stadium. At the back were playing fields stretching across four acres to the site of the 'Theme Park', which would be built at a later date. This area was marked as "Phase Two". Peter's problem was how to get the model up to 'Sky Mountain' as it would not fit in the Jag, and he did not want to damage the Rolls. This is where he did a very silly, in fact a most stupid thing. He called Vicki and asked her if she would come down to the Town Hall to give him a hand. His idea was that her old car would be the ideal conveyance for transporting the model. Vicki was under the impression that she was needed to help move some things around inside the Town Hall, and said, "No problem, be there in twenty minutes."

Peter said, "Great, and by the way, I will not be back for dinner tonight."

"Of course not" replied Vicki, "We are going out for my birth…"

But Peter cut her short by saying, "There's a special meeting at Sky Mountain tonight and I'll be sleeping over." He then put the phone down.

Vicki sat on the floor, she was trying to breathe. Her whole body was shutting down. Eventually she got up and walked to the airing cupboard, threw everything out and got in. She adopted the foetal position and stayed there until the evening came. She wanted to cry but the tears would not come, Peter had forgotten her birthday, she had

31

been betrayed. She was not asleep, but neither was she awake, she was suspended somewhere in space, she felt safe in her cupboard and would have stayed there but for the chime of the front door bell. She pulled herself together and stumbled downstairs. The bell rang again as Vicki opened the door to find an impatient Doris standing on the step.

"Whatever is the matter with you?" asked Doris, "You look like death!"

"I'm thinking about it," replied Vicki, "Please go away!"

"There's no need to be like that," said Doris, "I only want you to keep an eye on my house this evening. I've been invited to a bit of a do up at the Ski Lodge, something to do with regeneration." "As a matter of fact," said Vicki, "I'm going out tonight, I'm going to kill my husband!"

This last statement had quite an effect on Doris, who for the first and only time in her life was lost for words. Vicki slammed the door shut in her face, went to the drinks cabinet and took out a half bottle of whisky.

After a couple of swigs she felt better. She then walked in circles for half an hour around her kitchen hatching a plan. She might kill herself, but first she would take out her revenge on the Abbey Wood Centre, and as it had not been built, she would destroy the model. At nine it was dark enough to go. She put on Peter's old duffel coat, stuffed the remains of the whisky in one pocket, and all the pills she could find in the other. She jumped into her car and made for the Town Hall where she parked in the bay outside that was reserved for the Mayor. She was surprised that she could do this, and even more surprised to find that the place was deserted. She sat there for a few minutes wondering what to do next. She was hoping to embarrass Peter in front of his posh friends when she smashed up the model with her trusty hammer, then she remembered, he wasn't there. The hate drained away, the sadness returned. It was so heavy she could no longer bear it.

Unsure of what to do, she swallowed as many pills as she could before she started to retch, finished off the whisky, and made her way down to the river. As she stumbled into the water, she thought of Jamie.

"Oh God" she cried, "I'm sorry, I'm so sorry, please forgive me." It was the lowest point of her life, she would never sink deeper, and lucky for her, it was also the lowest part of the river.

CHAPTER EIGHT

"THE MEETING"

Peter was not too annoyed when Vicki didn't show up. He had a lot on his mind, June was coming in by train, she would stay the night up at the Ski Resort. As there were no trains from Liddingdale on a Sunday, he would have to drive her over to Preston to catch one back to Scotland. He instructed Bert, the chauffeur, to put the model in the back of the civic car, pick June up at the station and take them both to the hotel. The meeting was planned for eight, after a sumptuous five course dinner, paid for out of the council's emergency fund. The guest list included the whole of the town council, fifty other people from various committees, organisations, and quangos, plus a dozen creeping toadies from the local area, including Doris. The best way to describe this august bunch would be to say, "If there was a big trough of freebees to stick your snout in, this lot would be in front of you."

Bert picked up June from the station, where she insisted on sitting in the back of the limo that was already littered with little polystyrene houses that had come unstuck from the model. Peter had wanted Bert to take her to Preston the next day, but he had demanded double time. June studied the scenery as they left the town. Soon, she hoped, the Thompson's Empire would stretch to this ugly little place, then all those nasty little shops would close down and the whole place would be ripe for development.

She closed her eyes and imagined her 'megastore' dominating the riverside.

The guests started to arrive by mid-afternoon, choking the car park to such a degree that Inspector Angela Sadler (who was an invited guest) had to call her duty sergeant and ask for a couple of bobbies to cone off Old Dyke's Lane and put in a twenty mile diversion to create an extra car park. At five, there was a champagne reception in the Julie Andrews Suite followed by dinner in the main restaurant which was named the 'Piste - de Resistance'. By eight most of the guests had gathered in the upstairs lounge, known as the "Summit Room". Peter cleared his throat, tested the microphone with a quick "one two" and got down to business.

"Ladies and Gentlemen thank you so very much for attending this very special, in fact I might say extraordinary", (the joke fell flat) "meeting of the Liddingdale Town Council. Tonight is a very special night as we have as our guest Ms June Thompson of 'Thompson's Super Saver Stores', a lady who wants to bring retail to Liddingdale!" After some muted applause, Peter had to sit down for a couple of seconds, as he realised he had said the whole introduction without breathing. Suddenly he sprang up again, taking the audience by surprise, and said "I give you Ms June Thompson!"

Angela, who was sitting near the front, studied June with the trained eye of a police officer. Around fifty five she guessed, about twelve stone with a reasonable figure. Bust a little sagged with age and neck getting just a bit ropey. She could not make out June's hands which would be a dead giveaway, although she remembered earlier in the day that they supported at least eight expensive rings. It was the face that took most of Angela's attention, big, round, with a complexion straight off the farm. This girl may have worked hard to get here, but she had not travelled far unless the supermarket business was easier than the Police Force.

Angela was a bitch, she knew that, had to be to make Inspector by thirty five, but this lady charming, the socks off a load of small town freeloaders, she was something else. She was the only one in the room who had ever had to meet a payroll for a few thousand staff every week.

June gave a brief description of Thompson's operations and then asked the audience to turn their chairs round to the right and look at the wall where a large white screen had been erected. The lights were dimmed and the image of a huge building, a sort of cross between Windsor Castle and Battersea Power Station on a bad day, took up the wall. It spilled out each side of the screen and one distorted bit even crept around a corner, making an illuminated "way out" sign appear from inside one of the end turrets. "This," said June, "Will take up the land south of the river by the Town Bridge. In fact some of it will be built over the river!"

"You can't do that," shouted Joe Willmott, "It's monstrous, too big!"

The room descended into chaos, and it took Peter a good five minutes to restore order.

"You will all be able to have your say later," he said in a voice too loud for the mike resulting in a high pitched screech as feedback bounced around the walls. This had the desired effect on the mob, especially Joe, who would be deaf for the rest of the night.

June stood up, smoothed her dress, and with a smile that would melt an iceberg, said in a firm but very sexy voice, "It will fit!"

(Bet you've said that before dear! thought Angela)

"There is room, because we will not only use the Bowls Club site, we will knock down all those nasty old expired buildings between The Drove and Trinity Street."

"You can't do that!" cried Fred Downsworth, "My auntie lives there, number twenty two, it's historical!" This last remark brought a few laughs, mainly because the whole area was built on a swamp, where chronic subsidence had generated a big market for contemporary wallpaper.

"It is not historical," replied June, now in overdrive, "There's no conservation area to the south of the bridge! Thompson's will pay in excess of five million for the ground alone. We will build a new bridge, plant six hundred trees, make a riverside park, build two wine bars, a floral clock, and throw in a bus station with its own clock tower!"

June sat down to thunderous applause. Angela, who was now feeling sick, thought this girl could even make money as a madam in a monastery of ultra gay monks. Now it was Peter's turn. He described the Abbey Wood Project in detail, and asked everybody to have another look at the model downstairs, but not to touch it, as the repairs were not dry. Before he threw the Meeting open to the floor, he assured the 'Good Folk of our Beautiful Northern Town' that there was no problem with methane gas at Abbey Wood, the situation had been monitored by experts and there was no risk to the public. Building of

'Phase One' would start as soon as permission was granted and the funds were available. He finished with a flourish, which he had practised a number of times at home in the bathroom, by saying "Regeneration in Liddingdale where we care for the community!"

This was followed by loud applause, but not as loud or enthusiastic as June had received. Peter waited for the standing ovation, it didn't come. People started getting up and making for the bar.

Before the public could have their say, Harry Bains, Head of the Treasury Department spoke about the financing of the project, and the tough decisions facing the Council over the riverside site.

Angela had been after Harry for years, but up to now, he had been just a little too slippery. She knew that one day, like all greedy people, he would make a mistake. While Harry was talking, most folk were at the bar and didn't bother to come back. The people who voiced their opposition in the open part of the Meeting were outnumbered, and many of their objections were overruled. As Joe Willmott put it after six pints of Hardcastle's Old Wastewater,

"Harry Bains?"

"More like Jessie James!"

CHAPTER NINE

"THE DREAM"

By ten, the party was over for Angela. She slipped out through a side door into the car park, had a word with the Constable on duty, then walked down the drive to try and locate her car. After ten minutes she was well on the way home, when she suddenly turned right at The Drove Crossroads and made her way into town. She held no loyalty to Liddingdale, her heart was set on promotion to higher office in a bigger place, but for some reason, she didn't like the idea of a megastore dominating the riverbank. Angela was from 'Down South' and wanted to go back. It was grim 'Up North'.

As she approached the Town Bridge, she suddenly pulled the car into the kerb and got out. Although it was June, there was a chill in the air. She walked onto the bridge, the town was deserted. Saturday night in Glassville, she thought, fleshpot of the north! She stopped half way across and looked down into the dark water. Then, she saw a woman sitting in the river.

Vicki was in a room, it was a beautiful room, warm and inviting. It looked out onto a garden. Through the large windows, she saw that the sky was a deep red, and the colours of the garden were exaggerated, every thing was bright, as though under a tropical sun. She noticed that the door that led into the garden was open, and as she made her way towards it, she heard a voice, coming from a long way off.

"Please step out into my garden," it said, "We have been waiting for you."

As she came nearer to the door, she felt the warmth outside, not a searing heat, but a beautiful balmy all round warmth. She wanted to step outside, into the beautiful garden, but something was stopping her.

"No!" she whispered, "I want to, but I can't, I'm needed here."

"We need you," said the voice, "We need you for our garden."

Vicki felt her feet rise from the floor, and then she felt as though she was leaving her body behind in the room, she was floating towards the ceiling, it was the most wonderful feeling that she had ever known, she thought she might be dying and if this was death, there was nothing to be afraid of.

Leaving her body behind, she started to drift towards the open door, she wanted to go into the garden, but at the last moment said in a firm but gentle voice, "I am so sorry, but I can't, I am needed, I have to build my own garden here on Earth."

Vicki came to with a start and was violently sick all over Angela's frock.

"Are you all right Mrs.Smith?" asked Angela, who, despite her training, was shaking like a leaf.

"Never better," replied Vicki, "Never better. I've been to heaven!"

"What were you doing in the river," asked Angela, who immediately realised it was a silly question.

"Trying to kill myself," answered Vicki brightly, "And if you want to know why Inspector, I can tell you. My husband, his Worship the Mayor, who has his hand up every skirt in the parish, including yours, has forgotten that today or what's left of it, is my fiftieth birthday. He was supposed to be doing something special for it!"

Angela was taken aback by Vicki's comments, but pulled herself together and decided to take Vicki home.

"I don't think you had better drive", she said, "You might run into one of my boys." "Chance would be a fine thing!" said Vicki, "By the way, you smell of sick."

Angela was very impressed with Peter's house, for a man with no money and enormous debts she wondered how he managed to live like this. Vicki busied herself in the kitchen and made the Inspector a coffee.

"Is there anything I can do?" asked Angela.

"I think you have done enough already," replied Vicki, but there was no malice in her voice, in fact she had never been happier in her life. "You can have him," she said, "I'm finished with him. You can have the house as well, but be quick before the Bank takes it and can you pick up my car? I might need it tomorrow."

Angela Sadler, fast track superbitch with a housebrick for a heart, for the first time in her life felt a little compassion. It was as though a very small flame had been lit.It was not very bright yet, but it was a start. The road to Damascus was waiting beyond the dark horizon.

"What sort of Cop are you?" Vicki suddenly asked, her eyes very bright.

"What do you mean?" asked the Inspector.

"Good Cop, Bad Cop?" said Vicki in an unusual transatlantic drawl.

"I don't know," said Angela, looking at her shoes.

41

Suddenly Angela took a small card from her coat. "Take this," she said, "It's my home number. Next time you're going to jump in the river, call me."

"Why?" asked Vicki.

"Well," said Angela, with the merest trace of a twinkle in her eye,

"I might join you."

CHAPTER TEN

"ROVER'S RETURN"

Sunday morning held the promise of a fine day. The sky was cornflower blue, unbroken, except for fluffy clouds, perched high on distant peaks. The 'Resort' was certainly living up to its name. June was packed and ready to go by breakfast. Peter took longer, he had been bad in the night. He was not much better when he swung the Jag out of the car park. June was bright as a button, looking forward to a scenic ride over the Pennines. Peter, who had the mother of all hangovers and a dodgy tummy to boot, headed for the M62. They drove in silence for an hour, June deep in thought, Peter counting every mile. Suddenly, on the Manchester Ring, Peter said, "I'll have to stop."

"That's ok," said June, "We've plenty of time, a coffee and a sticky bun would be nice."

Peter opened his window and breathed in deep gulps of motorway air.

He pulled into Bolton West and parked in a bay near the door. He couldn't wait for June, throwing her the keys, and saying, "Give me a few minutes."

On his own he mulled over the events of the previous day and by and large he was pleased with himself, he would book a table there for the following Saturday, which he was convinced was Vicki's birthday. When he felt a little better, he looked around for June, who was in the shop. He watched her buying things, a key ring for her

43

father, fudge for her mum, a tiny teddy for a niece, a magazine for her PA. She looked sad, she had everything, she had nothing.

At the station, she kissed him on the cheek, and before going through the barrier said, "I'll give you a call mid week, there are some people in Glasgow who might be interested."

"Interested in what?" asked Peter.

"You don't remember do you?" she said, "Last night I told you there are some guys who are interested in that land at the back of the church."

"The allotments?" asked Peter, who could not remember much that had happened after the presentation.

"That's right, they could regenerate that area with the two hundred bedroom hotel that you'll need when Phase Two kicks in."

"But that land belongs to the church it was where part of the Abbey stood!"

"And the church needs about a million for the restoration of that big window that's cracking up."

"You can't build there! People have been growing vegetables on that site for one hundred years."

"Tough," said June as she showed her ticket, walked through onto the platform, and was gone.

Vicki was having the time of her life. She realised that she would not be going to New York, so if Vicki could not go to Central Park, then Central Park would have to come to Vicki!

At eleven, two very young policemen brought her car home. She invited them in for coffee and they had a pleasant chat about nothing in particular. She told them about Central Park and one said,   "In that case the Inspector will have to provide a black and white Chevey with NYPD on the side."

His mate said, "You only want a Chevey so you can drive it to the levy."

"The day the music died," said Vicki.

"Yes," they said in unison, and sang "American Pie" getting the words all wrong.

Vicki started to design her Park. She found the best place to do it was in the airing cupboard where she rigged up a little light. Around half an hour after the two lads had left, Angela called to check if her car had been delivered.

"Yes," said Vicki, "and thanks for those two lovely boys! Now Angela, may I call you Angela? I've something to tell you, it's very important. I'm going to build a park, like the one in New York, but bigger, I'm going to build it in Liddingdale!"

"Great," replied Angela, "Have you a location in mind?"

"Oh yes my dear, I'm going to build it on Abbey Wood!"

"Right," said Angela, lost for the right words, "Why don't we meet up for a drink sometime?"

"Great" replied Vicki, and then said with a funny American accent, "Look Toots, sounds good, be there, but can I take a rain check?"

"You sound a bit strange, where are you?"

"In a cupboard."

When Peter arrived home around four, he couldn't find Vicki. "Where are you?" he called.

"Up here dear," she replied, "I'm in the airing cupboard drawing up plans for a new park, like the one you are not taking me to see in New York."

Peter sat at the kitchen table with his head in his hands. Oh God, he thought to himself, June wants to knock out half the town, and my wife's designing a park in the airing cupboard."

At six, Peter asked for his tea. "Not tonight dear," said Vicki, who had no intention of letting on that he had missed her birthday, "I haven't time I'm going out."

"You will have to walk then, because my car is blocking your car in," Peter called up the stairs with a smirk on his face. Like a bolt of lightning she rushed down, grabbed his keys from his jacket pocket and was out of the door, her last words being "I'll take your big pussycat tonight dear!"

Vicki headed down to the Engineer's Arms. She had heard that Jessie was often there and she wanted to tell her about the dream, as Jess was known to have a window into the world beyond. She had only been inside the Welder's Bar once before and that was with Peter before he had rose up in the world. To her disappointment the place was empty except for little Allan, shy, spotty and nineteen.

"Hello Mrs Smith," he said politely, "Do you remember me? I was your paper boy you gave me wine at Christmas."

"What do you do now Allan?" asked Vicki.

"I'm waiting to go to college in September. I'm going to be an accountant."

"Very nice," said Vicki, "Can I buy you a drink?"

"Coke please," said Allan. "Did you hear the rumours? I'm not really gay."

"Oh that spot of bother over at Halifax," said Vicki.

"God!" said Allan, "It'll be in the papers next!"

After about an hour and five cokes, Vicki suddenly said, "Would you like to have sex with me?" Allan was not at all surprised. He looked more worried than surprised.

"You are a real woman aren't you Mrs S?

"Well that's for you to find out," said Vicki, "And if you are a good boy, I'll let you drive my big black pussycat!"

"Ok," said Allan, who had clearly been propositioned before, "As long as we don't have to drive anywhere near Halifax."

CHAPTER ELEVEN

"BIG MICK"

Vicki arrived home around midnight, Peter was asleep upstairs as she crunched up the drive. Before she turned in she slipped a small silver key off Peter's key ring. The night proved to be a bad one for her husband, with numerous trips to the bathroom. At seven next morning Vicki was in the kitchen making him a fry up which she took up to him on a tray. The sight of this produced another sprint across the landing and much heaving and moaning. When he was safely under the duvet Vicki told him that she would be out for the morning. Peter said he may have to stay at home as he did not feel well. "Never mind dear," said Vicki, "I'll leave some thin soup in the microwave, just give it three minutes."

"Where the hell are you going on a Monday morning?" he croaked.

"Things to do, people to see, places to go, and I'll see if Jess will do my hair, hasn't been right since I sat in the river." Peter pinched himself, hoping that he was having a bad dream.

"Don't worry my brave little soldier," said Vicki, "I'll take my car, and by the way, if you do feel better, my boyfriend made a bit of a mess on the back seat last night, might want to give it a scrub, forgot to take his boots off. Peter rolled over and thought that when strong enough, he might look up homes for the insane in the 'Yellow Pages'.

Just as she was going, the phone rang, it was Jamie.

"Hi Mum," he said, "Sorry about Saturday, I was going to phone, but I had an accident."   "That's ok," said Vicki, "What happened are you alright?

"I'm ok Mum, the health and safety officer would not allow us to build the bridge as we might fall off and break something or get a rope burn or a splinter."

"So what happened?"

"We went blindfolded quad bike racing round the field instead. They said it was great for team building, there's no 'I' in team you know!"

"So what happened?"

"Well it was ok at first, but then I missed a bend and went out onto the road."

"What happened!"

"The bus is a right off, but I'm alright and the passengers are ok, except for one woman with a broken arm, I've been in hospital, bit of concussion. I'll be going home today, the bus driver said it was his fault as he did not anticipate a blindfolded quad bike driver coming at him at thirty miles an hour out of a farm gate!

"Give my love to Linda."

"Will do Mum, happy birthday, love you, and remember there's no 'I' in team!"

"Oh yes there is my son!" said Vicki quietly as she put the phone down, "Oh yes there is!"

Vicki drove into town and dropped the little key off for a duplicate to be made. She then went round to the Bella Vista. Jessie was sitting in one of the chairs, they were not busy. When she saw Vicki she asked what had happened to her hair. Vicki told Jess about the weekend, except for the bit with Allan and the Jaguar. Jessie was sympathetic and very interested in the Heavenly Garden. "You must do this," she said, "Your old man and his mates want to ruin this place, they've been trying to get me out for years, want to build a multi-storey hell hole of a car park."

"I hate men," said Vicki.

"No you don't, you can't hate anyone."

"Why?"

"Because you were put on earth to build a garden and you can't build anything without seed."

Jessie suggested that Vicki should join the "Girls" on Wednesday down at the Welder's, and then said, "Let's go shopping! Mandy can cover any emergencies."

"What about my hair?" asked Vicki.

"Well it's been in a fire and it's been in the river, we might find a cement mixer we could shove it in!" said Jessie, "Anything would be an improvement!"

Peter was not well. He was on the bed staring at the ceiling when the door bell rang. He wanted to say go away, but it came out as the sort of squeak a mouse might make when being run over by a steam roller. The bell kept chiming and after a minute or two, Peter stumbled down the stairs and threw open the front door. Harry Bains stood on the step in a crisp blue suit matched with a large silk tie from Amsterdam. He could have been big in conservatories and double glazing.

"You look rough," he said.

"I feel rough," replied Peter, his normal voice returning, "I think it was the prawn cocktail."

"Never have it, not since Bridlington," said Harry.

"The herring was fine, are you going to let me in? I think it's starting to rain."

Peter ushered him into the lounge where they sat down opposite each other, either side of a large expensive looking fireplace.

"Where's the little woman?" asked Harry.

"Gone to hell I hope, that fire did something to her," said Peter, "Anyway what do you want?"

"That's why I'm here, I think we should clear up the fire damaged part of the site before the press start poking about. The Police and Fire Department say its ok, so I think we ought to put the security fence back. Do we still have that fencing we pinched up at the yard?"

"Yes we still have it, but do you think it might still be dangerous up there?" asked Peter, showing a rare stab of conscience.

"Nah," said Harry, "If it ever flares up again, we'll blame it on Tom. How did you keep him quiet by the way? He's got a mouth like the Mersey Tunnel."

"Angela Sadler," replied Peter.

"You can be a very naughty boy sometimes," said Harry.

Having a sensible conversation with another member of his own sex revived Peter's spirits a little and he offered his visitor a drink.

"Sorry Harry," he said, "I seem to be out of scotch, how about vodka?"

"Vodka's fine," said Harry, "Now back to business, I think we ought to put something up there to make it look we are ready to bring in the builders."

"We don't have any planning permission yet!" said Peter.

"Foregone conclusion," said Harry, "Just a matter of time." He saw the look on Peter's face and then said quietly, as if the house was bugged, "Phase One is not on the landfill, the reclaimed land will be used for the playing fields which carry no weight, it's all marked out on the plans."

He then produced a small pocket calculator and punched the keys with his big fleshy fingers.

"The landfill is over 500 metres from the road, that's…" but he couldn't get the answer, so he said "Well it's getting on for half a mile."

"How did you ever get a job on the Council?" enquired Peter.

"I'm finance, not surveying," said Harry.

Peter was not satisfied and asked, "The Bowls Club, was that on reclaimed land?"

"Just on the edge, sort of," said Harry.

They had another couple of drinks, Harry stood up and looked out across the front lawn. Rain was coming down in sheets, bouncing off the roof of his van parked in the road. Peter stood up, as Harry looked as though he was preparing to leave, and out of the blue said, "We ought to make a statement up at Abbey Wood, we ought to put a great big sign up there telling everybody that we mean business, a great big sign with great big letters!"

"Saying what?" asked Harry.

"REGENERATION!" cried Peter in a high pitched squeak, "REGENERATION FOR ALL!"

"Nobody goes up there," said Harry "Nobody will see it!"

"Big Mick!" he squeaked, "We'll use Big Mick!"

"And who the hell is Big Mick?" asked Harry, "Some bloke from Rotherham?"

"The crane up at the yard," replied Peter, "It's not high enough, but I bought another old crane for scrap some years ago, same sort, we can go up over a hundred feet, and sling a banner from the jib."

"Sounds dangerous," said Harry.

"No, no, no, not at all," replied Peter, "We can jack it up section by section, we'll pile drive RSJs thirty feet down in each corner, and we'll light it up at night!"

Harry, not convinced, said "I've got to go, make sure you get that fence back up this week." As he walked out into the rain he turned and said, "By the way, what were you doing last night, parked up round the back of Badger's Wood?"

CHAPTER TWELVE

"HEN NIGHT"

Vicki returned home mid afternoon. It had stopped raining and Peter was washing his car when he saw her struggling up the drive with half a dozen shopping bags.

"What have you got there?" he asked, "In all those bags?"

"Clothes," replied Vicki, "I'm going down the Welder's on Wednesday evening, girls night out. I'm going to dress up a bit."

"Some girls!" said Peter, "A load of ugly old slags more like!"

"Well you should know dear," said Vicki, "Seeing as how you have slept with most of them."

Peter watched as his wife tried to get through the front door in one go. Vicki put some of the bags down and said, "Oh by the way this credit card does not work anymore," and threw it at him.

"So where did you get the money for all that?" he shouted, his voice starting to go squeaky again.

"With the money that I saved for my trip to America," she said.

Peter tried to grab her but forgot that he was holding a fully charged sponge of car shampoo which temporarily blinded him. At that moment his mobile rang, and quick as a flash, Vicki picked it up off the front step.

"Harrow," she said, in a strange oriental voice, "This is the Chinese Laundry, what you want?"

"A broad Scottish accent on the other end said "Is that you Peter? You sound a bit funny."

"It's your trollop," said Vicki handing him the phone.

"Are you ok?" enquired June.

"Fine," replied Peter, "I've been having problems, I think it was the prawn cocktail."

"More like the ten pints of sump water."

"It's Waste Water, made from the pure springs of the Blackdyke Ditch up other side of Dingly Dale, Hardcastle's finest, first brewed 1792!"

"Ok cut the history lesson, look I've arranged a meet for Wednesday, place near Hexham called the 'Bear Forest Resort' sort of cowboy town with log cabins, looks fun, some sort of timeshare, bring your boots and lasso!"

"Sorry June," said Peter, "Can't make it, something's come up."

"Ok," said June, sounding a little downcast, I'll try for next week."

"That should be fine," said Peter.

"Good," said June, "I'll see what I can do, these guys from Glasgow don't like to be messed with." And with that, she put the phone down with a loud click.

Vicki made Peter a robust dinner which he managed to eat without too much trouble. After washing up, she disappeared for an hour, and just as Peter was dozing off in front of the TV, she burst into the lounge looking like a cross between buffalo girl and a scarecrow. Peter stared in disbelief. She was wearing a very tight pair of wranglers, high heels, and a blue checked shirt that showed off most of her limited cleavage. She did not wear a hat, but she had dyed her hair a strange colour. A large blue ribbon was strangling a docked pony tail at the back. Peter did not quite know what to say or do when she sidled over and said in an unusual drawl, that was more Norfolk than Nevada, "Howdy Partner, can I park my chassis on your lap, or is it reserved for one of your other old moo cows?"

When Vicki woke the next morning, Peter was already gone. He wanted to sort out Abbey Wood before the end of the week. His staff were busy all day shuttling between the yard and Monk Lane with the wire and posts that he had taken the opposite way a few weeks before. He also got his friend, Bill Crab, to take parts of the crane over to the site in his old truck. Things were going well, the whole of the council workforce was up there leaving road works and maintenance suspended all over the town. If the weather held out, he would have 'Big Mick' up and ready by Saturday. He thought of telling the local rag, but decided not to push his luck. On Wednesday they had pile driven the RSJs deep into the ground and they were being bolted to the base and first tier of the crane. Four big cables from a tug boat were also supporting the tower that started to rise above the waste land. The jib, with the slogan 'REGENERATION' in large black letters was already fixed and climbed higher with each extra tier. This was dangerous work, the guy in charge was a black eyed mutant with extra fingers called Boko who had worked on travelling fairs and in the circus all of his life. He knew a thing or two about large unexpected erections in remote places.

On Wednesday evening Vicki booked a taxi to take her into town. Peter was not back, as the work on 'Big Mick' was going on well into the night. In the taxi Vicki phoned Angela and invited her to join the party. Angela said she was working but would try and get down later. When Vicki arrived at the Welder's, the place was already full. She made her way to the bar and found Jessie who kissed her in a sisterly way, and then introduced her to the gang. The only man Vicki could see was little Allan sat on his stool in the corner. "Be back in a minute," she said to Jessie. She went over to Allan and bought him a coke. "You were good," she said, "And you told me you had never done it before."

"You weren't so bad yourself Mrs S," replied little Allan with a smile.

"Well I was a bit rusty, but it soon came back to me," said Vicki.

"Thanks Mrs S." said Allan, who was eyeing up a large woman who looked as though she had just completed the late shift in a steel foundry, "It was not as difficult as I though it would be, automatic cars are quite easy to drive when you get used to them!"

Angela arrived around ten. As she entered the room, everyone stopped talking and stared at her.

"There's a funny smell in here," someone said.

"Yes," said another, "I can smell the Old Bill or is that the Old Bitch?"

"Come on, come on," said Angela in her 'come on, we know you did it' voice, "I'm a working girl as well!" instantly regretting saying it and wanting to die in some dark corner of a far off land.

This was greeted with howls of laughter and she was escorted to the bar. From this point on the evening was a great success. Bill arrived just after Angela, and was introduced to all the ladies by the Inspector, who knew each one by name. When they got to Roger, 'she' said, "Come off it Inspector, you know I'm Petula on Wednesday and Saturdays!" On seeing Allan, Angela said quietly in his ear, "It's ok over at Halifax, they are not going to press charges, he's done it before."

During the evening. Vicki told everybody about her dream for a new Park and what a nasty person Peter was. Some of the girls got a bit upset, as they thought he was lovely, but by and large they all warmed to Vicki. When it was time to leave, Vicki offered a lift to Angela and Jessie in the taxi, but Jessie said she would walk Bill home, which was room 301, three floors above. Vicki had not been used to hard drinking, and in the taxi became morose, saying to Angela, "It's just a silly, silly, stupid dream. I'm just a daft little cow with a face like a gone off pudding in a closed down cafe!"

She then continued, "I'm a Goliath against the Daniels, no that's not right, I'm a feeble stick that's blowing in the wind, I'm a, no you're a Rolls Royce Angela, with a blue light, while I'm a Detroit Dustbin, I'm an Angel and you're a um, Angie, may I call you Angie? Please will you take me home now? I don't think I'm capable of walking and I think Peter, who is the Mayor you know, well yes you know of course you know because you've been intermittent with him now and then, well I think he's going to kill me!"

"You're not crap," said Angela firmly, "I'm crap, I'm a crap cop, I'm a crap mother, you didn't know about that did you? I'm a crap daughter, I'm a crap human being! I'm so deep in the dog's do I couldn't see the daylight with a periscope, but I'll tell you something, you're going to do it, I don't know how, but I know you're going to do it, and I'm going to help you."

"Thanks Angie," slurred Vicki, "I'll make sure Peter doesn't drag you down the toilet with him."

As the taxi pulled out of the car park they saw Allan walking home. "Stop!" Vicki instructed the driver, and then shouted through the open window, "Allan, come over here!" She pulled him close, and as drunks tend to do, breathed on him and said, "Now you can handle my big black Pussycat, how would you like to drive a real sports car?"

CHAPTER THIRTEEN

"MAKING PLANS"

Angela helped Vicki out of the cab and paid the driver. She dragged an unwilling Vicki up the gravel drive, leaving two perfect tram tracks in her wake. At the door Angela rifled Vicki's handbag for keys. When she found them there were only three on the ring along with a scruffy plastic fairy. Angela felt a pang of sadness, a fifty year old woman with just three keys. She chose the most likely and put it in the lock. Like everything else in the house, it worked perfectly. After dragging Vicki into the kitchen she thought of making a pot of black coffee, but Vicki was well gone. From upstairs she could hear Peter snoring for England. She propped Vicki up against the fridge and whispered, as if to a child, "Sleep tight," then went out into the still night. Under a star-filled sky, Angela walked home. She had a lot to think about.

Jessie took Bill by the hand and steered him to his bedroom door. Bill was not sure what would happen next which was quite exciting. "Not tonight," said Jessie, "We don't have to rush these things at our age, let's make do with a cuddle."

"Would you mind if I kissed you?" asked Bill.

"Go on then," said Jessie in a matter of fact way, as if she snogged old blokes in hotels most nights of the week.

Bill leaned forward to give her a quick peck, Jessie

grabbed his face, pulled it towards hers and kissed him hard on the lips.

Although it came as a bit of a surprise, Bill soon got the hang of it and did his bit.

"I enjoyed that, you're a bonnie lass Jess, that were a good kiss," said Bill. "Better even than them big native women I met in the jungle. That were lovely," and then he said, possibly because of a gallon of Hardcastle's Wastewater inside him, "That were even better than a plate of 'Yorkshire Faggots' on a Friday night at the 'Strangled Cat' in Dewsbury! Now I want to do something and it might not be to your taste, but I have to do it."

"Are you a bit kinky?" asked Jessie.

"Don't be daft lass, I'm from Stannington!"

"Well you'd better get on with it. I've got to go to work in the morning."

Bill kissed Jessie hard on the lips, he opened his slightly, pushed her head back and put his tongue into her mouth and rolled it around a bit. He made a quick withdrawal and said "Thanks."

"What was that all about?" asked a breathless Jessie.

"I had to know, you see. I've got this phobia, I just had to know."

"About French kissing?"

"Don't be daft!"

"What then?"

"I had to know if you had your own teeth, can't abide false ones!"

"All mine and paid for!"

He kissed her again and said, "Are old people supposed to do this sort of thing in hotels?"

"My first husband was a sex maniac," she replied. "He was up for it until his ninety fifth birthday, then, all of a sudden that was it and he left me alone, got a taste for mushy peas and origami."

"So what happened?"

"I had enough of it, so I broke it off."

On Thursday and Friday Peter and Boko worked from dawn to dusk putting the finishing touches to 'Big Mick'. By Friday night it was finished and resembled a cross between the Eiffel Tower and a huge pylon with another pylon sticking out horizontally just before the top. Hanging from this latter bit was a twenty five foot banner proclaiming 'REGENERATION!' in big black letters on a white background. The only things missing were the four big arc lights and generator which Boko had managed to borrow from his mates on the fair, along with a five hundred gallon diesel tank. All this was arriving early on Saturday. The deal was completely unknown to the Inland Revenue.

Vicki had also been busy, making numerous trips into town to visit the Library. On Friday afternoon, she went to the office of the 'Weekly Word' and poured over the archives. Her evenings were spent sitting at the kitchen table, drawing up colourful plans in felt tip. The new park was to be named 'ELYSIUM', simply because she liked the sound of the word. With all this endeavour Peter had to make do with ready meals. Boko came home with him in the evening and Vicki provided food for both of them along with massive lunchboxes each day. After dinner, Boko would sit in a corner like some wild animal let out of its cage. Peter had provided him with an old caravan from the scrapyard, and this was parked in the field on the opposite side of Monk Lane, as it was too big to get on site. It had an old fashioned, gipsy style clerestory roof with a peak. The other workers on site were very curious about Boko and his unusual physique. Because of this, the caravan became known to all as the 'Dome of Discovery'.

Bill was kept busy sorting out Enid's little bungalow.

He had agreed to meet Jessie on Saturday for a drink. She suggested going to the 'Glass Blower's Tavern' as it had a more intimate atmosphere and a carpet. On Friday Bill moved into the bungalow, he thought he might stay there for a short time.

He could show prospective buyers round and also get to know Jessie better. He called his neighbour in Stannington and asked her to keep an eye on things for the next couple of weeks. He called his bank and found that the money from the sale of the garden centre had gone through. He was quite a rich man. Jessie knew nothing of his past, what he did in the Army or his life with Mary, the long hours in the steelworks, and the successful garden centre. He decided to be more open in future. He wondered about her husbands, was it all made up? He had started telling stories of his life in the jungle and they were getting more and more outrageous, he didn't mean to do it, but all those husbands were starting to get to him.

On Saturday morning Vicki woke to the chime of the front door bell. She found a bouquet of flowers on the doorstep. The card read, "From your ever-loving Peter x x x." She gave a wry smile and dumped them in the sink. On the kitchen table there was a birthday card in a box. It's too late Peter, she thought, it's much too late my dear, I've

63

moved to a world beyond your comprehension. She looked at her face in the bathroom mirror, it was now more like sago with big uneven dollops of plum jam, she couldn't care less, and said out loud "Sod the eyebrows, I'll go naked, it's my second birthday this year!"

When Peter arrived at Abbey Wood the generator and fuel tank were already there. The fair boys were unloading the arc lights off an old Foden along with about two hundred miles of rough looking cable and sticky tape. Within minutes Boko and his mates had the electrics rigged up. Boko then climbed the tower like a monkey and bolted a huge red light on the top. He was down in seconds and Peter suggested they had a test run. Boko, a mutant of few words, said robot fashion, "Look at that, a Gardner 6LX!" They fired her up and the lights came on. One of the fair boys said to Peter, "Listen to that, sweet as a nut, that's music! Better than all your Beethoven!"

Peter paid them off and said to Boko, "Stay on until after the 'switch on' tomorrow and oh yes, I've got a job for you tonight." As he drove home Peter got a call from June who told him that the 'Meet' had been arranged for Wednesday, and could he stay over for a few days?"

"Okey Dokey," said Peter as he drove along without a care in the world.

Far out to the west, beyond the Irish Sea and the Plains of Athlone, beyond the twelve Pins of Connemara, ominous black clouds were drifting in from a dark and distant Atlantic.

On Saturday afternoon Peter was all sweetness and light, he even offered to cut the lawn.   When Vicki asked him what he would like for his tea, he said, "Surprise! I'm taking you out to dinner!" The surprise turned out to be the Ski Resort which Vicki had expected. What she had not expected was that he had made it a foursome, as he did not want to have to talk to his wife all evening. The two stooges were Doris, and Boko, who was wearing tight leather trousers and a red shirt, open nearly to the waist exposing a plantation of curly black hair. The Black Forest, Vicki thought and wondered if he might have a couple of cuckoo clocks hidden in there.

The dinner was not a success. Doris sat opposite Peter looking into his eyes making gurgling sounds like a hippopotamus having an enema. Vicki ate everything she was given and then had seconds. She looked round the table. Peter and Doris were leaning across towards each other, their noses almost touching, like some grotesque Puppet Show. For a split second she felt sorry for them, they were ugly people trapped in an ugly world. She wondered why they were so selfish, perhaps it went back to the Garden of Eden. There would be no serpents in Elysium, she would make sure of that. She looked across to Doris, lonely, growing old and fat, was she ever happy?

Had she ever run through meadows in spring and made love in the long grass? Was she happy with her husband Dave, before he went off to Llandudno to run a B&B with Barry from the fish shop?

She thought about Jamie and Linda, both now thirty something, no kids not even a cat, old before their time, living on an executive estate in a house designed by a computer, golf on Sunday, matching sweaters, cocoa before bed. Jamie going on pointless weekends to get motivated in some dreary hotel. She looked at Boko, trapped in a body that was different. People in the restaurant were staring. What was wrong with being different? Jesus was different and they murdered him. Now two thousand years down the road, in a ski resort with no snow, people stared at her face because it upset the safe normality of their empty lives.

Boko had that same frightened look that he had at her house. She felt that he did not like to be indoors near to people, he was wild, untamed but not dangerous, a big black spider hiding under the sofa, until you go to bed and it's safe to come out. His eyes flicked around the room, every now and then he looked towards the door. Vicki stared back at him, she was in control. At nine, a birthday cake arrived with one candle. "Make a wish," said Peter. Vicki turned her stare on him, it penetrated his very soul. The waiter removed the candle and cut four tiny slices, arranging them in a pretty pattern on a small plate. Vicki stood up and offered it round the table. Boko and Peter both took a slice, but Doris refused. Vicki then gave the waiter the plate and said "There you are, take that home for your dog." She looked across at Boko, he turned away, looking for a place to hide, but she followed him with her eyes. Helpless, he gave in and stared back. A lamb looking into the eyes of a tiger.

On Sunday morning Peter went to check on Big Mick, he wanted to make sure everything was ready for the 'switch on' at dusk, when the whole town would see that the council was ready.   Soon the money would come rolling in, some of it into his pocket. Boko had gone, he had taken the keys and the TV. People were driving past looking at the crane and the slogan, one man stopped and took a photograph. A guy came up and asked, "What's all this about, is somebody having a laugh, is it something to do with modern art?"

"It's Regeneration," said Peter

Vicki picked up the phone, "Hi," said Angie, "I really wanted to speak to Peter."

"He's playing cranes up at Abbey Wood," replied Vicki.

"Look," said Angie, it's not really a police matter, but I need to speak to him."

"Can I help?" asked Vicki.

"It's that blasted crane, Big Mack."

"Big Mick."

"Oh yes, Big Mick, well it's an eyesore, we've had dozens of complaints, they want to know if the Council have gone bonkers, what's it all about?"

"Search me."

"Well will you tell him that I may have to put one of my boys up there tonight, there could be trouble, stay at home Vicki, don't get involved."

"No chance of that Angie, I couldn't give a donkey's doo dah, anyway I'm much too busy.   Now listen, I want you to do something for me, do you remember Bill from the other night?"

"Nice old guy with Jess, yes I remember him, I introduced him to les girls."

"That's the one, now listen, there's more to our Bill than meets the eye, I've been down to the local rag and found out that he's a war hero!"

"Did he get the VC or the DSO?" asked Angela, trying not to laugh.

"Now listen smartypants, I found an article from 1958, a

piece about his wedding, he married Mary Maine from Corporation Street, daughter of Fred and Enid. There's a bit about him, fought bravely in the jungle etc. etc. But it doesn't say what he actually did, can you dig around for me?"

"I think you're doing pretty well on your own Sherlock!"

"Don't get funny, this is important, now listen, I will be busy this week, don't call, I'll give you a bell on Friday."

"Ok Cap-it-tan," said Angela, "But don't go too far in that old car of yours."

"Why?"

"We can't find it on our database."

There was a pause and then Vicki said in a quiet, soft voice, "Was it a boy or a girl?"

"Pardon?"

"The baby, what was it?"

"It was a little girl," replied Angela.

"What happened?" asked Vicki.

"I gave her away, held her in my arms, she had beautiful blue eyes, wide apart, and perfect little hands and feet, I held her for a short time, and then they took her away."

"I'm so sorry," said Vicki, close to tears.

"Don't be," replied Angela, I had my career to think of."

"Ok," Vicki's voice changed back to PMT mode, "Friday, I need to know, find out about our old soldier, and Angie, if you have any trouble with my old man tonight, lock him up!" And with that she slammed the phone down.

It broke the glass on the coffee table.

A slightly stunned Angela walked to the window, opened it and shouted to the world, "The worm has turned, Vicki Smith will build her park in this godforsaken place, I know she will!"

"Is that you Inspector?" The voice came from Detective Sergeant Parrot, having a crafty smoke in the yard below.

"Oh Hi Beaky," said Angela, "How do you fancy a trip to Acapulco?"

CHAPTER FOURTEEN:

"A WALK IN THE PARK"

The rain arrived on Sunday afternoon and by four it was coming down in sheets, driven by a strong westerly gale. That evening Peter drove his big black car to Abbey Wood. Monk Lane was deserted except for one police car with a young PC hunched over the wheel, deep in a paperback. Peter drew up tight to the fence. He pulled the collar of his raincoat up around his neck and stepped out into a puddle. Armed with a large torch he opened the flap and delved into the intestines of the control box. After five minutes or so the big Gardner coughed into life and then settled down to a nice even pace. Peter slammed the four big levers down, there were some sparks here and there at first, but after a few seconds, the tower was illuminated. When he returned to his car, the young policeman had gone.

Jessie and Bill were having tea in the bungalow, she had spent the day with Bill giving the place a 'woman's touch' as he was going to see the Estate Agent the next day. They sat at the ancient well scrubbed table, like an old married couple. Bill for his part had touched her whenever he got the opportunity and saw some new bits when he was holding the stepladder, as she painted the ceiling. Up to now she was still like the Amazon, largely unexplored. He had his canoe at the ready, but it was still on the bank, expecting to be launched at any time. The previous day, they had fish and chips at the 'Glass Blower's which was rather swish for Liddingdale as you could sit out on the pavement with a nice view of the old coalyard. In the afternoon Bill drove Jessie up onto the moors. They sat and talked, Jessie going on about her husbands, Bill servicing whole villages of big grateful women in the jungle.

After a time they fell asleep, later being woken by a young couple in a bright red car. The youngsters got out and made for some stunted trees in the distance. "Bless," said Jessie. In front of them the whole of Greater Manchester was lit up like a Christmas tree. Jessie pointed out Mossley and Oldham, Stalybridge and Shaw, it was the most beautiful sight that Bill had ever seen.

Then she spoilt it all by saying, "Over there is Ashton, my third husband once drove a trolleybus in the town, some nights he would come home with a ten foot bamboo pole!"

"Time to go!" said Bill. On the way back he said, "At least we can say we've slept together, and by the way, if we ever did get married, which number will I be?"

Peter told Vicki that he would be away from Wednesday to Saturday, he was going to a seminar near Milton Keynes to 'access ways to regenerate the systems of corporate management and find solutions to future trends for financing the executive status of modules in multi-matrix bipolar organisations with solutions in efficient tidal flows for the end user'.

"What does that mean exactly dear?"

"Regeneration!"

"Sounds like bullshit."

Peter had no intention of going to Milton Keynes. He

was driving north to Hexham, to do a deal with the guys from Glasgow, sleep with June, get drunk, and play cowboys.

On Monday morning Vicki went to town and picked up the extra key that had been made for her. She then made a visit to the Bella Vista for some major construction work.

"Will my face ever recover?" she asked.

"I don't know," replied Jessie, "But whatever happens, it will be your face."

"That doesn't make sense," said Vicki.

"I do tend to talk a lot of crap," said Jessie, and they both laughed.

"Do you love him?" asked Vicki.

"I don't know," replied Jessie, "He keeps going on about all those women in the jungle. What if he got the pox, how long does it take to wear off?"

Vicki couldn't answer, she was laughing with tears rolling down her uneven face.

"Jess," said Vicki after a long period of silence, "Would you come out for a drive on Thursday? You can bring Bill if you like. Also, I need little Allan, will you ask him to pop round and see me Wednesday afternoon? It's very important, I must see what Central Park looks like in the flesh."

"Are we going to New York?" asked an excited Jessie.

"Don't be daft girl!" cried Vicki, "We are going to Birkenhead!"

A sheepish Allan rang Vicki's bell, the door opened and he was pulled in. "I am so glad to see you darling!" said Vicki, "I want to introduce you to Monica." They went out to the garage where Vicki pulled a big dusty sheet away to expose a car, "This," she said to Allan, "Is Monica!"

"Wow!" said Allan, "A Morgan, a real one, not a Kit Car, a real Morgan, British Racing Green, strap over the bonnet, Wow! Where did you get it?"

"It belongs to Peter," said Vicki, as she gave him the new key. "It's his pride and joy, the only lady he will ever love, and you, my son, are going to drive her all the way to Birkenhead for me."

"Where did he get it from?" asked little Allan.

"It was my Dad's," said Vicki, "Always wanted one, saved all his life for a Morgan, bought it two years before he died, after the illness struck he would just sit in her, touching the wooden steering wheel, staring ahead down a road to nowhere. When he died, I gave it to Peter.

Allan may have been a callow youth, but he knew his cars and on inspection said, "A Plus Four, early sixties I would say, optional wire wheels, TR two litre engine."

"It might be a bit special," said Vicki, "Dad said it was a sports tourer, and it had a sports engine."

"It must have the 2.2litre Triumph lump, sports tourer means it's a four seater by the way."

"Can you get it to go?" asked Vicki, "It's been standing there since Christmas."

"Don't see why not," said Allan, "But it will need a bit of a run, the tyre pressures need checking, and of course it will need fuel and that could be a problem."

"Why is that?" asked Vicki, thinking what is it about men and cars?

"We need to know if it will run on unleaded, I don't mind taking her around the block, but a journey to the

Wirral and back, well I'd like to know how hard her valve seats are."

I only wanted him to drive the bloody thing, thought Vicki. "See if it goes," she said, "I'll look for the paperwork." She raided Peter's desk, it was locked, but a screwdriver and hammer fixed that. She walked back to the garage where Allan was working under the bonnet, "Problems?" she enquired.

"Not really," said Allan, "Battery's been taken out, but there's one on the bench and I've stuck it on a high charge, let's have a cup of tea, then we'll see if she goes, she's got almost a full tank, but the tyres look a bit suspect."

While Allan drank his tea, Vicki rifled through a whole wad of papers, "Is this it?" she asked, "Exchange cylinder head, there's a lot of jargon." Allan grabbed the invoice and quickly surveyed it, "Ah yes!" he said, Birkenhead here we come! At this point the phone rang, it was Jessie, who wanted to know if Allan had turned up.

"Yes, he's here," said Vicki, "And he's getting my new car started, are you on for tomorrow?"

"Yes please," said Jessie, "Just one thing, any chance of going to New Brighton?"

"Yes that's ok," replied Vicki, "There's something I must do on my own, Allan can take you and Bill and pick me up on the way back, why New Brighton?"

"My last husband lived there," said Jessie, "Worked on the Tugs in Liverpool with Billy Fury."

Oh my God! Thought Vicki, and then asked, "Is your boyfriend coming?"

"Yes he's up for it, and insists on paying for the refreshments."

"Just one thing," said Vicki, "Don't go on too much about Jolly Jack Tar, Bill's very fond of you, I don't want a domestic in a small car on the East Lancs Road!"

By the time Vicki returned to the garage, Monica was outside and running, "I might have to weaken her mixture," said Allan, "But she looks in good shape Mrs S, just like you."

"You certainly know how to charm the ladies," said Vicki, "I want you to take her for a run and top up the tyres and the tank, you can stay here tonight, if you like."

"If I can bring my teddy," said Allan.

"You can wear mine," said Vicki, "Now off you go here's some money for fuel and a road atlas."

Vicki went indoors rolled up her 'Master Plan' and tied it with a wide red ribbon so it resembled a huge diploma. She threw a few things in a bag, in case she never came back.

Thursday turned out to be a beautiful day, so they decided to have the top down. Vicki did not like the motorway, so Bill sat up front with Allan and navigated a more interesting route. Because of the wind noise, the girls had to shout to the boys on the flight deck. After Rochdale, Jessie said, "Why do you need to go to Birkenhead?"

"I have to see the park," said Vicki, "The one I'm designing for Abbey Wood is based on Central Park, New York, I can't go there until I've got shot of Peter, so I'm going to Birkenhead which is the next best thing."

"I'm afraid you lost me along the way," said Jessie.

"Look," said Vicki, "In 1847 Birkenhead Park was brand new and one of the first municipal parks. It was designed by a guy called Sir Joseph Paxton, he designed the original Crystal Palace for the 'Great Exhibition' in London.

"Is this going to be a long story?" asked Jessie.

"Look you asked me and I'm telling you," said Vicki, "New York wanted a park and two guys, a writer called Fredrick Law Ormsted and an English architect called Calvert Vaux developed a plan called the 'Greensward'. Fredrick toured Europe in 1850, looking at parks and things, and when he saw Birkenhead Park, he was very impressed. So Birkenhead Park was a sort of model for Central Park, although it was more an idea that a blueprint if you get my drift?"

"I don't believe that anybody could be called Calvert Vaux!"

"Not even one of your many husbands?"

"Shut up!"

"Now, now girls," shouted Bill from the front, "It's a smashing day, and young Allan here is a very good driver, we'll be crossing the Mersey soon, and then we'll be there."

They crossed the Mersey and the Ship Canal on that graceful steel arch at Widnes.

"I remember the Transporter that stood here before this bridge," said Bill. "You had to wait your turn and pay, there were only ever three in the country, only two now.

"I know it's a silly question," said Jessie, "But what are you talking about?"

"It's a bit complicated for a lass to understand, but if you ever come to Stannington, I'll show you my model Transporter Bridge, I made it out of Meccano in 1953!"

"You'll be getting a smack before the end of the day," said Jessie.

"Promises, promises," said Bill.

Allan, with Bill's help, had no trouble finding the park, where they dropped Vicki and her plan off at the grand entrance. Bill was impressed and asked Jessie if he could go with Vicki as he had been to New Brighton before. Jessie said, "No, Vicki has to do this for herself." When they had gone, Vicki walked into the park, found a bench, sat down, and unrolled the plan. When you see pictures of a place, when you study maps and read books about somewhere you think that you know it, but you don't. Everything that Vicki saw was alien, this was not New York. This park was beautiful, the most beautiful park that she had ever seen. One day, when Peter had gone, when she was free, she would go to New York and see the Boathouse Café, where Harry Met Sally, and take photos at Tavern on the Green that was used in Ghostbusters, but all that belonged to New York, not Liddingdale or Birkenhead. She rolled up her plan, placed it gently in a litter bin, and tied the ribbon to a tree. She walked lightly, as if on air, around the park.

People stared at the little lady, with the funny face, dancing on the grass.

Bill did not want to go to New Brighton, he'd been there before, not long after Mary died. It was a day trip from Chester where he was visiting an old friend from the Army. He had taken the train to Liverpool, it was a cold winter's day and on the spur of the moment, he decided to go to New Brighton. When he got there a mist had crept in off the sea and he spent an hour in a damp café, before returning on the next train. He was sure that Jessie had never been there, but she had told a story, now she had no choice but to keep up the pretence. Neither of them were talking when they arrived in the town. Allan, who was quite grown up for his years, said that he would give them some space, and take Monica, who he had fallen deeply in love with, for a spin.

They crossed the road and Bill sat down on a bench, looking out to sea. Jessie knew that something was wrong. "Please leave me here for a while lass," he said, close to tears, "I just need to sit here quietly for a time."

"I'll go and do some shopping," she said, "Bring you back an ice cream."

"That would be nice," said Bill.

Jessie put her hand on his shoulder, "I feel your pain," she said.

When she came back, Bill had recovered, "Sorry," he said "I just needed some space, as young Allan would say, he's a lovely lad, I wish I had been blessed with a son."

"It's really nice here," said Jessie, "I've been watching the boats."

Bill got up and took Jessie's arm, "Would you care to walk along the Prom with me madam?" he asked, "The ozone is exceptionally fresh today, let's go and have a big plate of black pudding!"

They found a smart café and had a splendid meal followed by two enormous mugs of very hot and strong tea. "When I was here last, it was not long after Mary died, it was winter, cold, wet, I sat in a café and wrote a poem, I have a copy of it somewhere in a drawer at home," said Bill.

"I'd love to hear that, I didn't know you were a poet," said Jessie.

"I've been trying to remember it, but it's morbid, it's all so long ago, in the past, best forgotten."

"I still want to hear it," said Jessie, "Have a go. It doesn't have to be word perfect."

Bill stood up, the café was empty, he cleared his throat, turned and faced an old sepia picture of the New Brighton Tower on the wall, "Here goes," he said.

"Cold wind from the river,
Running through the streets,
The town is clean and quiet,
And bright, but no one speaks,
Shops with shuttered windows,
Silent ships at sea,
Shapes deep in a café'
Huddle over tea,
No one shows their anger,
No one shows their pain,
And I don't care if summer,
Ever comes again."

"That's beautiful," said Jessie, but Bill was running out through the door laughing "Come on slow coach, I'll race you to the sea, last one's a sissy!"

On the way back, Allan got stuck in the rush hour traffic and it was past six when they picked up Vicki at Birkenhead. The trio were apprehensive as they approached the grand entrance to the park, but they need not have worried, she was smiling and jumped into the front seat of the Morgan. Out of breath, she said in her strange American accent, "Let's head for home John Boy, get this eighteen wheeler rolling, lets see black coal from the stacks. Put the hammer down, slam her in the Georgia overdrive and burn rubber, hold on to your rubber chicken!"

"I think you may be in the wrong movie," said Allan.

"Why is Bill in the back?" she asked.

"They have been a bit funny since leaving the seaside," said Allan, "They keep sighing, I don't think we should take them to New Brighton again, he's started to dribble."

"They're in love, Bozo!" said Vicki.

The traffic did not ease for some time, and when they found an empty road, they were lost. Vicki was not well travelled, apart from a honeymoon in Spain, she had never been further than Blackpool, it was starting to get dark and she was afraid. They stopped for petrol, and while Allan was filling Monica's tank Vicki went for sandwiches and asked the attendant where they were. She came back to the car and informed them that they were on the Cheshire Plain near some towns called Nantwich, Northwich, and Middlewich."

"But W H I C H ONE are we near?" asked Bill, followed by an unwanted "Ho, ho ,ho."

"Let's stop for the night!" said Jessie.

CHAPTER FIFTEEN

"THE CHERRY TREE"

They sent Allan back to the shop. When he returned he had a big grin on his face. "There's a motel just up the road," he said, "Five minute drive!" After a good ten minutes they saw a green sign proclaiming "MOTEL 400YDS ON RIGHT". Allan drove slowly and sure enough there was another sign which was by a gap in a large hedge. He turned Monica and headed down a gravel track that ran between an avenue of dark shapeless trees. The second sign had a bit more information on it, as it told the world (if the light had been working)

"CHERRY TREE COMMERCIAL MOTEL" and in smaller letters underneath,

"Restaurant – Colour TV – In House Video". "What does commercial mean?" asked Bill.

"It's an overnight stop for Reps and Business Travellers," said Allan, "I bet the car park is stuffed with company cars"

"What's 'In House Video'?" asked Bill.

"It's not for you," said Jessie, in a schoolmarm tone, "It's for adults."

"I hope it's not like the Bates Motel!" said Vicki, growing more edgy by the second.

"Well if it is, don't use the shower!" said Allan.

"That's not funny," said Vicki.

"Perhaps after we get checked in we could go over to

the old house and have a word with mother," said Bill, just before Jessie kicked him hard on the shin, a difficult manoeuvre in a Morgan.

When they eventually got to the Motel, they found, as Allan had predicted, a good number of work stained 'Repmobiles' each loaded to the gunnels with samples and catalogues. As soon as the car stopped, Vicki was out, breathing in deep gulps of cold night air.

Vicki was shaking, her world was closing down, this was not planned. She was lost, in the middle of nowhere. Jessie ran across and grabbed her, "What's up?" she asked.

"I'm losing it!" cried Vicki, this shouldn't happen, we should be home, safe, I should have died, I had the chance, I should have died!"

Jessie grabbed both her shoulders and shook her, "Don't talk like this Vicki," she shouted, "You had a second chance, you got out of the river!"

"I should have died, I should have died, I'm losing control!" sobbed Vicki.

Jessie slapped her face and Vicki went quiet. "That's better," said Jessie in a soft voice. When Jessie looked at the other two she saw a nodding donkey and a startled rabbit. "Keep those expressions boys," she said, "And come with me, Vicki you come too and let me do the talking, let's have a bit of fun, and if we can't get in, I'll drive you all home!"

"You can't drive," said Bill.

"I told you to shut up," said Jessie.

They all trooped in through a door marked 'Reception', this was in a large ugly building up a slight slope, all around were smaller versions which Vicki presumed were the bedrooms, she hung on tight to Allan. Inside at the opposite end to the door was a large built-in desk, behind which was a dark frayed curtain. Jessie went up to the desk and rang a huge brass bell with more force than it was designed to take. A pale looking old lady appeared from behind the curtain and took a big black book out from under the desk. "Sign here," she said in a matter of fact voice.

Jessie said in a perfect West Country accent, "We only want one night," to which the old lady replied, "Nobody stays longer than one night."

"We need two of your finest chalets my dear," said Jessie "For my family."

"That will be £50, money up front, Chalets 13 & 14, breakfast from seven," the old lady replied in a mechanical voice as though the Cherry Tree Motel had to cope with four misfits from Planet Loony every night of the week.

Jessie dragged Bill out towards the door, Vicki and Allan followed. At the door, Jessie, now building up for an Oscar, said in a loud voice, "Thank you so much my dear, we aint never been in a motel before av we Faaaarther," looking at Bill, who was nodding like a donkey let out to do a nativity play. She continued, "This errr," pointing to Vicki and Allan, "Be our Molly and Cousin Tom, we all be cousins where we come from in 'Downey Uppham'. Molly asss to sleep with Tom case eeee goes a bit funny in the night!" The old lady showed no signs of alarm, she was obviously used to dealing with inbreeds, she did however stare at Vicki's face for a split second. Outside, they collapsed in fits of laughter, even Vicki was smiling.

The chalets resembled log cabins and were quite cosy, each fitted with a modern en suite bathroom. Vicki put her small bag on the floor by the sink. She was the only one of the group who had any toothpaste, so she put two dollops on the sink and gave the rest to Jessie. Allan was tired and went straight to bed, "Are you ok Vicki?" he asked, it was the first time he had called her that.

"I am now," she replied, "I think Jessie might be my guardian angel, I'm ok now, back on track.

"I'm glad," said Allan, "Well good night then."

"I'm not finished with you yet my boy!" said Vicki.

"Not tonight Mistress I'm too tired!" said Allan, as he pushed his head deeper into the pillow.

"Do your parents know where you are?" asked Vicki.

"I told them I was driving an old lady to visit her sister in Whitley Bay."

"Well you'd better call them and tell them the old lady had a fall and you are staying the night!"

"Ok Mrs. S will do," said Allan and grabbed his Blackberry from the bedside table.

When she had settled into the sheets, Vicki woke Allan up and said "I know your Dad, he's a farmer."

"An agriculturist, grows stuff for specialised markets, not a proper farmer."

"Have you got any empty buildings on the farm?"

"One or two, can I go to sleep now?"

Vicki shook him and made him sit up. "Take this," she said and placed a large key in the palm of his right hand. "This key," she continued, "Is the spare key to my garage, the Morgan is still in my name, before long Peter will go bust and we may lose the house, when that happens, I'm off! I have a little money that my Gran left me, I want to see New York."

"What's this got to do with me?" asked Allan.

"I'll tell you what it's got to do with you," said Vicki, "If Peter goes down the pan, I want you to take Monica and hide her on the farm for a couple of years. If you do that I will see my solicitor and make sure that she's yours when you are twenty five."

"You don't have to do that," said Allan, "Yes I love her, I love her deeply, but she's yours."

"I want to," said Vicki, "And by the way, drive very, very carefully tomorrow."

"Why's that Mrs S?" asked Allan.

"Because none of us are insured to drive her!" said Vicki.

Bill went for a walk round the car park, there was not much room in the back of the Morgan and he needed to stretch his legs. When he got back to the chalet Jessie was already in bed, the sheets up round her neck. "You were quick," he said, "Are you as nature intended?"

"Well I'm not a bloke if that's what you mean!" she said indignantly.

"I mean are you in the all together?"

"Of course not, I have my vest and pants on!"

Bill went into the bathroom and cleaned his teeth with a finger, as he had no toothbrush. He had a wash and emerged into the bedroom in a pair of ancient boxer shorts.

"Are you leaving them on?" asked Jessie. Two seconds later they were off and flying over her head. Bill did a bodybuilder pose and said, "Look at that, almost a Chippendale!"

"Don't be silly Bill, come to bed." said Jessie.

Bill moved in close, but Jessie pushed him away, "What's up Jess?" he asked.

Jessie started to cry, "It's been quite a day," said Bill, "First me, then Vicki, now it's you having a blub, have I caused all this?"

"Course not!" said Jessie, "It's me, I've deceived you!"

"What ever do you mean?" asked Bill.

"Well it's all these husbands, truth is I've never had a husband, I'm an old maid, I took you to New Brighton on false pretences, I upset you, and you were so kind."

"Well if that's all it is, come here!"

"No Bill, I want to get it off my chest, the reason I could do that Somerset accent tonight was because that's where I come from. My Dad was the Butler on a big estate, Mother was the Housekeeper. They were very strict in those days. I never had a boyfriend until I was twenty.

Anyway, no boy was good enough for me, and by the time my parents retired I was thirty, and in those days if you were thirty and single, you were on the shelf, and I've been there ever since."

"Well I'm glad it's all out in the open," said Bill.

"Let me finish please," said Jessie, "I got a job working in the telephone exchange, it was the Post Office in those days, and I got a transfer to Bradford. Later I took a hairdressing course and ended up in Liddingdale. I've had sex, I'm not a virgin, but I must say I've never enjoyed it very much, messy business, like making marmalade, never had one of those thingimywhatsits."

Bill stared at the many cracks in the ceiling, trying to find something to say. Eventually he said, "Those big women in the jungle, they didn't exist. I just got a bit upset when you kept going on about your husbands, so I made them up, I only ever had that sort of thing with Mary."

Then Jessie started a conversation, which Bill would remember for the rest of his life.

"Bill," she said, "When you were in the jungle, what was it like? Have you ever told anybody?"

"No lass," he said "I never even told Mary, I might have if she'd lived. It was bad, if you were not there you can't really imagine, people dying, blown to bits, your friends, young lads, just kids, I can't tell you Jess, because I can't come to terms with it, not now, not ever, even after fifty years.

Jessie leaned over, put her arm around him and drew him very close, but Bill pulled away. Then quite suddenly, he said, "I want to tell you something Jess, I want to tell you, I've got to tell somebody before I die, I'm sorry it has to be you, because I love you, and you shouldn't be burdened with it."

"What is it Bill?" asked Jessie, "Come on let's have no secrets."

There was a long pause and then Bill said, "I killed a man, it was him or me, and I killed him, he were just a lad, like me at the time, I killed him and I think about him every day."

Jessie grabbed hold of Bill's big hands, "Go on," she said softly, "You need to let go."

"It was in the jungle, hand to hand stuff, all of a sudden there he was, we faced each other, he lifted his gun then he hesitated, just for a split second as though he knew he couldn't do it, murder another human being. Well I was scared, I fired and he went down. The bullet went into his chest, there was not much blood but I could see the pain in his eyes, I can see those eyes now in this crummy hotel. When they have those parades and they march up and down with their medals and flags, I don't go, because I don't need one day a year, I think of him every day, and when it gets bad, I go down to the bottom of my garden and light a candle for him in an old tin can. He had a Mother and a Father, perhaps he had a sweetheart…" and then his voice trailed off and he buried his head into her chest.

Jessie cradled him in her arms, as a mother cradles her baby.

Vicki was up at dawn, she crept out of the chalet and climbed a small hill behind the Motel. There was a wood with a meandering path that led to open country. She looked down on the earth and the rolling fields, it was all man-made. Left to God it would be a wilderness, is that what she was trying to create, a sort of wilderness? What was a park anyway? It was going to be much more difficult than she thought, messing around with the natural order. She knew that this funny little planet, so far out from the centre of the spiral and so alone, needed a bit of help. On her way back she looked out for the cherry tree and mentioned to the others that she couldn't find it. At breakfast, which was surprisingly good, Vicki asked the old lady "Where is the cherry tree?" to which she replied,

"I chopped it down five years ago."

"Do you have an axe?" asked Allan sarcastically.

"No," she said, looking him straight in the eye. Then she winked and said,

"I have a chainsaw."

CHAPTER SIXTEEN

"LOSING CONTROL"

At ten on Friday morning, they left the Cherry Tree Motel and headed northeast. Allan drove very carefully, and at one point Vicki asked him to get a move on. Jessie and Bill were very quiet and Vicki was a little worried about them, but each time she looked round, they were holding hands and smiling. Allan complained that there was no c.d. player or radio in the car, but with the noise from the engine and the rush of the wind it would have been very difficult to listen to music. "We don't need a radio!" said Vicki, and without warning sang the first line of 'All around my hat,' in a strong clear voice. Jessie came in from the back with the second, then Bill with the third. They sang the rest in harmony. This was followed by 'Molly Malone', 'Green Grow the Rushes' and 'There's a Small Hotel', which they changed to Motel. "Where the hell was that small Motel?" asked Bill, "Which 'Wich' was it?"

"I don't think it was Middlewich," said Jessie, "And I don't think it was Nantwich," said Allan.

"Well," said Vicki, "Why don't we call it GRANNY'S TWICH!"

After a pleasant three hour drive they arrived back in Liddingdale, where Allan stopped in the market place. From here they went their separate ways, Jessie to her small flat above the beauty salon, Bill to call in at the estate agents, and Allan to the bus station. Vicki drove Monica slowly back to Abbeyfield Drive, where she reversed the sports car carefully into the garage. Later, she covered her up with the dust sheet, and locked the garage door. Around mid afternoon, Vicki called the Police Station and left a message for Inspector Sadler.

An hour later Angela called back, "Hi Angie," said Vicki, "Have you found out anything about our soldier boy?"

"A bit," replied Angela, "Seems he was a hero, saved a few lives apparently, I've made up a file, I can drop it round if you like?"

"Yes please," said Vicki, "I could do with some company, come round for dinner tonight, I'll do a special 'Hot Pot', and before you ask, Peter's not here he's getting motivated in Milton Keynes!"

"Great," said the Inspector, but I can't make it 'til eight, there's a bit more about Bill though, we found out that he may be rich, he had a very successful garden centre on the outskirts of Sheffield, it was in the centre of a big road interchange, he called it 'Plant Island'. He sold it a few months back. He has no criminal record, but he's done his bit for the community, been in the Round Table, Lions etc. We are still trying to find out if he's a Mason."

"They wouldn't have my old man!" said Vicki, "He can't be trusted!"

"He's been known to roll up his trousers though!" said Angela, "But to be serious for a moment, where the hell is he?"

"I've just told you, Milton Keynes," said Vicki.

"Milton Keynes my Aunt Fanny!" said Angela, "Look I need to speak to him, we've had a barrow load of complaints about that eyesore up at the landfill, when is he coming home?"

"Sometime tomorrow," said Vicki, "But I've no idea of the time."

Angela brought a bottle of wine, and after dinner they sat either side of the fireplace. Vicki was studying Bill's file intently, "What exactly are you looking for?" asked Angela, "Perhaps I can help?"

"I want to know what he did in the Army," said Vicki.

"Well you know what he did, he was a soldier."

"Yes, but what sort of soldier, what was his job?"

Angela grabbed the papers from Vicki's hand, sorted them and then handed one back, "There," she said, "Read that."

"I don't understand any of this," said Vicki, "It's too complicated."

"It means," said Angela, "That he specialised in explosives."

"Did he now," said Vicki, "Did he indeed!"

Before she left Angela gave Vicki a bunch of keys. "These came from that old caravan where Boko was sleeping, he dropped them round to the station. We used one of the keys to get into the compound and stop that generator, it's been running since Tuesday, at least we will not have to look at that eyesore tonight!"

"Thanks Angie," said Vicki.

As Angela walked to her car she turned to look back at Vicki, "You are up to something my girl!" she shouted.

"What me?" said Vicki, trying to look like Pollyana on a Sunday school trip.

"Yes you!" shouted Angela, "Be careful, I don't want to fish you out of the river a second time!"

"I'll be ok," said Vicki, "I nearly went under last night at Granny's Twitch, but I'm stronger for it."

Angela turned her car in the road and drove away. When she got to the main road she said to herself, "Where the hell is Granny's Twich and why didn't Granny get some treatment for it?"

Just after midnight the phone rang, it was Peter. "Where have you been?" he asked.

"I've been working down Pump Lane, I've decided to become a prostitute."

"No one would want to pay you with a face like that!"

At one time, Vicki would have crumpled up on the floor, or made for the airing cupboard, but it had no effect on her at all. "Are you coming home sometime?" she enquired.

"I'll be back tonight, and I will want something to eat."

"What time? I need to know when to start cooking."

"Don't know," he said and tried to end the conversation, but Vicki was having none of it and told him that the Police were fed up with taking complaints. Peter then told Vicki that there was to be another meeting and a big splash in the local paper and some of the county papers about Phase One, the Theme Park, the Megastore, and the Hotel, with an extra bit by the Vicar of St. Mary's about how these schemes will save 'our wonderful church from collapse'. He finished off by saying that the money was there on the table and the rest was just a formality.

I'd like to know where this table is, thought Vicki, as she walked into the lounge, took his mayoral photo out of its frame and flushed it down the toilet. She then took the frame and smashed it to pieces with the poker.

The trip to Hexham had been fruitful the guys from Glasgow were keen to invest money in the new Sports Centre and the Theme Park. They liked the idea of grabbing the church land for a Hotel. June was ready to move as soon as the demolition orders could be obtained. Peter had something on most of the Town Council and some of the District Council, he also knew what the Vicar got up to with Mavis Shuttlecock and Bob Dewland on a Wednesday night behind the Fire Station.

The Bear Forest Resort, however, had been a bit of a let down, more 'Hello Campers' than chaps on cattle drives.

Peter was in good spirits as he drove back, the only problem now was to keep the Bank off his back for a little longer.

He did not want to lose the scrapyard as he had another four figure consignment due, but if the house went he could move in with one of his girlfriends, or even Doris. Vicki could go with the house. All this was swimming around in his head when he saw the car coming the other way on his side of the road. Instinctively he took to the grass and put the Jaguar as close to the trees as he could slicing off the door mirror in the process. He saw the driver, a dark shape behind the windscreen, he heard the blast of air horns from the truck that was being overtaken. He closed his eyes, the big car started to buck and pitch as it tore through the grass, the steering wheel was wrenched from his hand, but when he opened his eyes, the other car had gone, it was close, it had missed him by inches. He was now off the road heading for the trees. He grabbed the wheel and regained control, slowing to a crawl until his nerve came back and his legs and hands stopped shaking.

He was driving fast, heading for Carlisle. It was a good road with sweeping curves. The Jaguar devouring all before her, the sun streaming in between the pines. Then it happened. First there was a feeling of being unwell, something slight, understated. Peter felt as if he were not in complete control, the big cat was running away from him. He lifted his right foot off the throttle, but it made little difference, she was gliding downhill, racing on. Then for a moment, he felt as if he was not there. His left foot did not seem to work properly and his left arm was hanging down the side of the seat. He seemed to be coming and going and it was getting worse, he had to stop and get out, the car was taking over.

Up ahead he saw a blue sign indicating a parking area. With all the concentration he could muster, he steered the car in and bumped to a stop against a high kerb. The Jaguar was still in drive but he could move his right leg after a fashion, and moved his foot away from the throttle. He tried to put on the handbrake, but his left hand was dead. The sky fell in on him.

An elderly couple were having a picnic, he leaned against the steering wheel and sounded the horn. The old man walked over and opened the front passenger door. "Please help me," he said, trying to hold his head up, "I think I'm dying."

Vicki got the call at lunch time informing her that Peter was in hospital in Carlisle, he was stable after sustaining a stroke while driving on the A69. Vicki did not cry. She felt nothing but a little regret that things might have been better between them. She called Angela and left a message, then she jumped into her car and drove to Carlisle. At the Infirmary the doctors said he had a good chance of recovering, but it would take a long time. She asked to see him and they took her to a side ward where he was linked up to various machines. Back in her car she switched her mobile back on. Angela had called and asked if there was anything she could do. Vicki called back and said,"No, I'm coming home." On the motorway she suddenly wondered what he was doing on the A69.

Vicki got back just before dawn, and slept most of the day. At five she rang Jessie who offered to come round, but Vicki said, "No, it's not that he's here much anyway." Later, she went next door and told Doris, who got very upset. Vicki drove to Abbey Wood and looked at where her park would be, she also looked in the caravan. Boko had left it clean and tidy.

Around ten Angela called and offered to tell John Pender, Peter's deputy on the Council, what had happened.

"Thanks," said Vicki, "I'd appreciate that, and can you get hold of Allan? Tell him to come and take the Morgan, she needs somebody who will look after her"

On Monday she called the hospital, he was stable but paralysed down the left side. He could not speak, but was making a humming noise.

They would try and move him to Liddingdale Hospital if he made good progress. Vicki spent the next week, sitting in the caravan at Abbey Wood, dreaming of 'Elysium'. Some days she would walk around the site planning in her head the pathways, the lakes and ponds, the tea shops and bars. She built imaginary hills and valleys and then went back to the caravan to draw her plans on scraps of paper.

Only once did she cry, and that was for her Dad.

CHAPTER SEVENTEEN

"DOG DAYS"

The weeks after Peter's stroke were uneventful, which is a misnomer, as most weeks in Liddingdale are uneventful. The town's people seemed to like it like that. Peter's enthusiasm for regeneration had not rubbed off on the average 'Liddingite', in fact if it hadn't been for the crane at Abbey Wood, most of the natives would have never heard about "Regeneration". They didn't want a big sports centre, as the more sporty ones had a few indoor facilities down at the Football Ground. The club had done quite well over the years and had an impressive stadium. Liddingdale also had a Rugby Ground on the outskirts of town, and in Upper Dyke Lane there was a posh golf club that didn't admit estate agents or bus drivers. All in all the townsfolk were comfortable with their town, and the town was comfortable with them. They still had a rail link with the main Trans – Pennine Route and you could be in the broken spider's web that is Greater Manchester within the hour. Some folk worked in London and returned at the weekend, Liddingdale was fast becoming a Dormitory, or a "Bedroom Town", as Johannes, the one legged Dutch postman, aptly called it.

After a few weeks Peter was transferred to the local Community Hospital, a huge ugly1960's monolith on The Drove, to the south of the town. This hospital had a stroke unit where he made slow, but steady progress. The doctors advised Vicki to be prepared for the worst, which meant that he might never fully recover. His days on the Council were over. On the bright side he could not speak, so she didn't have to talk to him. Vicki was told that eventually he would be sent home, a future she did not relish and certainly did not plan for.

She had been told that they would send a nurse each day to start with. This was a life sentence that she could not endure. She had a park to build, but for the present there were bigger cookies to crumble and much bigger fish to fry in the kitchen of 17, Abbeyfield Drive.

As soon as her husband had left the scene, the full realisation of his debts fell on her. She was not stupid, she knew he was a waster and a crook, but that was his business until now. At the Bank the kindly Manager explained her situation. The mortgage had not been paid for months and the overdraft had been spent. Peter had asked for more time, and because of his standing it had been granted, but now the Bank had no option but to close all accounts. This did not come as a great shock to Vicki as she had a little of her Gran's money left. The lenders allowed her to stay in the house for a full three months and she was grateful for that. Another piece of luck was that Bill took Edith's bungalow off the market and offered it to Vicki. Bill had let his house in Stannington and was living with Jessie in the flat above the Bella Vista.

The biggest problem however was 'Smith's Recycling", a major part of the town's industrial scene employing over twenty people. This was shut down a week after Peter was admitted to hospital, Vicki had learned what she already knew, that it had been on borrowed time for some years.

Before the Receivers were let in Angela sealed off the whole premises and started an investigation. Dave, the foreman, was arrested and later released on police bail, as evidence was gathered. It was only a matter of time before they came for Peter, and in some ways Vicki thought it might have been better if he had cashed in his chips on the A69. One evening Dave turned up at Vicki's house. He gave her a large envelope stuffed with money.

"Don't ask questions," he said, "Hide this, it will keep you going for a while,"

As July gave way to August a hot spell developed bringing long dry days that did nothing to lighten Vicki's spirits. Although she was innocent, Vicki could not develop her friendship with Angela, so she came to rely more and more on Jessie and Bill, who came round for dinner most Sundays and stayed until late. Towards the end of the month Angela called and asked Vicki to meet her for tea in 'Betty's' the following day. Vicki, who lived part of her life in the movies, was quite excited as she took the train, while Angela drove to Ilkley. Vicki disguised herself with a large hat, which made her stand out somewhat from the usual crowd of old ladies. One thing she could not disguise was her face, now starting to look like coconut icing over a bakewell tart, which blended in quite nicely with the scones and jam.

Angela told Vicki of the problems they were facing at the yard, there was some really nasty stuff hidden away and Dave had confessed to taking very hazardous waste up to the landfill. The main problem for the Police was that Peter had kept no records, and could she have a look round Vicki's house sometime? Vicki told Angela that she could have the house, as it was not hers anymore. They both laughed and got stuck into a truly memorable tea. On the train home, Vicki wondered if she would ever build her park. Was the land poisoned? What could she do?

The train dived into a long dark tunnel. When it emerged into the sunlight she looked out across the rolling hills, and knew exactly what she would do, once the Dog Days of August drifted into the sharp days of September. She needed help, it was dangerous, but it was the only way to build Elysium on Earth.

With Peter out of the way the Regeneration Plan stagnated. June pulled out, she could not work with Harry Bains, who she detested. She took her Megastore elsewhere.

Joe Willmott quickly pushed for a preservation order on the land and buildings south of the Town Bridge and the reinstatement of the bowling green. John Pender, the 'stand in' Mayor, was an ex civil servant, dull as ditchwater, the sort of chap who keeps all his socks in the same drawer and drives a Rover 75. His idea of a good day out was to monitor the traffic lights outside Lancaster Town Hall. John Pender was everything that Peter wasn't, strong, solid, and totally useless. He was not very keen on the Sports Centre Scheme and was happy to forget about it for the time being. The Glasgow boys dropped out much to the dismay of the scheming Vicar and his collapsing church. The Theme Park was dead in the water. All that remained was a rusty old crane and a banner that now read 'GE E T N' due to high winds on August Bank Holiday.

On the first day of September Vicki had a visit from the

Vicar of St. Mary's, who offered his condolences and hoped her husband would soon be home. He kept asking if Peter could talk, and Vicki had the feeling that he wanted something. She made a pot of tea and steered the conversation towards life and death, mainly death, which seemed to make the Vicar very uncomfortable. "I've seen the Garden of Eden," she said brightly, "God wanted me, but he's going to let me stay here a bit longer to build my Park." At this, the Vicar motioned to leave, but Vicki pushed him back into his chair. "Do you believe in Heaven?" she asked, "Do you believe Peter will burn in Hell for what he's done?"

"Well," said the Vicar. Looking like a condemned man, "It's all a matter of interpretation you must have faith my dear only God knows all the answers! These near death experiences are just dreams. God has a plan for us all."

"And what's the next bit of his plan?" asked Vicki, now firmly in the Captain's seat.

"We do not know, we have to believe, we are in his hands!" said the Vicar, making for the door.

As he neared the door Vicki blocked his way and said, "Are you going to visit Peter this week?" to which the Vicar, now looking like castrated old bull on its way to the slaughterhouse replied, "Yes, and I will pray for him every day."

Vicki grabbed the Vicar's lapels with surprising force and drew his sallow face close to hers. "Well when you have seen Peter and tried to find out where all that nasty unchristian money is, go down to Ward Five, you will find a lady sitting by the bedside of her five year old son, who will be dead and in his coffin by next Friday."

She pushed him hard against the wall and said,
"If you decide to pray for her, ask God why her son has
cancer."

CHAPTER EIGHTEEN

"WOW!"

In September, Bill took Jessie to Marbella for two weeks. While there, he asked her to marry him. She told him she would, but not yet. She had the Bella Vista to consider and she did not want to live in Spain, it was too hot and she loved England. When he asked her where she would like to live, she said, "By the seaside." Bill understood and was quite happy to bide his time, she was a good cook and she was letting him have a bit more of the physical side of things. Jessie loved Bill but she did not really enjoy sex, which she considered was like Haggis, nice for a change, but you didn't want it every day. Bill also seemed to huff and puff a bit which she supposed was normal, although they didn't mention it in the romantic novels that you could buy at the station.

The first Sunday after they returned from holiday was spent at Abbeyfield Drive. During the afternoon, when Bill had a snooze in the conservatory, the two girls had a heart to heart. Jessie told Vicki the intimate details of her love life, while Vicki explained her present financial situation. She said nothing about the envelope full of money. Vicki confessed that the Park might not be built, as she had no idea where the money would come from.

"Have faith," said Jessie.

"That's what the Vicar said!" replied Vicki.

After tea, Jessie watched 'Songs of Praise' on the TV. Bill and Vicki sat on the patio.

Vicki turned to Bill and said, "I want to ask you something, will you be my Dad? as I don't have a Dad any more."

Bill's eyes filled with tears, "I would be honoured," he said.

They sat there holding hands listening to the music coming from the house, and then Vicki said in a quiet voice, so quiet that Bill had to lean down close to her face, "I am going to ask you to do something for me, if you can't do it I will understand and I promise I will never mention it again. I know you are a brave man, I know what you did in the jungle, I also know that you were an expert in demolition, explosives and the like." Bill made to reply but Vicki stopped him by touching his face and then running her fingers through his thinning hair. She stood up and walked onto the lawn well away from the house, he followed her and when they met, she dropped the bombshell.

"Dad," she said, "You know the crane at Abbey Wood? Well I want you to blow it up!"

Bill stared back in disbelief. When he had gathered his wits he said. "All that stuff in the jungle was over fifty years ago, what makes you think I can still use explosives?"

"Because you are an expert, I've seen your file, I needed to know, I think you were sent to help me. I know it's not easy, we might get caught, we might get killed, but nobody else will get hurt. Don't answer now, think about it, let me know in a few days." Bill grabbed Vicki by the hand and marched her back to the patio where they sat down, although Bill was shocked, he was intrigued. "Tell me your plan," he said, "You must have something worked out."

"Well first of all you have to get a bit of group one," she said.

"What's that?" asked Bill.

"Well you know," said Vicki, "Dynamite or cordite, gunpowder, I don't know, you're the expert. I'm just going on what they say in war films."

"And where do I get it from?" asked Bill.

"That's easy," said Vicki, "You have an old Army friend in the demolition industry."

"Ok," said Bill, rather enjoying the scenario, "What now?"

"You go up there at night and stash the material in the caravan. I'll get Allan to move it down to the bottom of the field, out of harm's way. Over a few nights you bury the explosives round the foundations, I'll give you a key, and then you get hold of one of those fancy detonators that are activated by a radio signal. On Guy Fawkes Night you go up there, make sure that nobody is around, and go to the caravan. At eight you punch in 00000 and BOOM! Everybody, including Inspector Sadler, will think a firework has ignited Peter's gas filled rubbish tip!"

Bill sat there and stared at his new daughter, he had to admire her imagination, "I'll think about it," he said, "But it's not that simple, I've got to get the stuff, I'm a bit rusty. What if it didn't go off?"

"Well," said Vicki, "If it doesn't go off. I'll confess to everything and you've never been rusty in your life!"

"That still leaves the problem of getting the stuff, it's expensive."

"I'll give you a thousand cash, there's more if you want it."

"And where do I get it?"

" Chalkie White, still does a bit of blasting with his son, old mate of yours, lives just outside Scarborough. I rang him, said you might be up there visiting friends this week, said you might pop in, he said he'd love to see you, talk about old times."

On Monday Vicki made a visit to the hospital. Peter was in a wheelchair trying not to dribble.   On the way back she popped into St. Mary's, the Vicar was nowhere to be seen. She sat for a while staring into the gloom, then she turned and looked at the Great West Window. A great calmness descended upon her. She heard a man's voice. He had a soft voice, it was not from the local area.

She turned to look at the stranger, he was middle aged and dressed in casual clothes. "Isn't it wonderful," he said, "Do you know that is the largest west window in England, that's on a parish church of course, but I think Bath Abbey has the only one that contains more glass."

"I have known it all my life," said Vicki, "In Liddingdale you either love it or hate it, some say it's garish, I love the colour, only our local glass can absorb the light like that."

"You have a great understanding of the world around us," said the stranger, "What happened to your face?"

"I was in a fire," replied Vicki.

"Is that why you sit here?" asked the stranger.

"I sit here because I want to build Elysium," said Vicki.

106

"You will," said the stranger. When Vicki looked round again, he was gone.

The Liddingdale Window was commissioned in 1850, and took the Victorians just two years to construct. Where Bath and Tintern have delicate tracery, Liddingdale has big brash stone arches between the glass panels, giving those, even with poor eyesight, a good view of Jesus and friends. At the very top with his head almost touching the apex, is a Hollywood Jesus, life size, looking down on his companions who get on with their day to day tasks in neat rows. At the very bottom is a Victorian workman standing by a huge kiln with a stylised version of St. Mary's in the background, looking a bit like a castle. In 1958, there was a minor earthquake, not one pane of glass was damaged. The Vicar may have been worried about it, no one else was.

When Bill told Jessie that he was going to Scarborough she insisted on coming along. Bill took her up to 'Oliver's Mount', where they sat by the War Memorial and had their picnic lunch. Later, Bill drove Jessie down to the Spa and dropped her off by the beach.

She told him that she would walk from there to the North Bay and take tea at Peasholm Park, she would wait by the entrance, so could he give her a call when he was on his way? She did not want to hear all about the war in the jungle. Bill drove out to Eastfield, which had grown somewhat since his last visit.

Chalkie was glad to see him and the two old veterans relived their Army days. Later, in Chalkie's garden Bill slipped a piece of paper into Chalkie's hand, "I want some stuff," he said. Chalkie looked at the list neatly written on the paper and took in a deep breath, exhausting it in a silent whistle.

"What ever do you want this for?" asked Chalkie, "Are you going to have a party?"

"Maybe," said Bill.

"I don't know," said Chalkie, "This is dangerous, and it will cost, "I don't know, I don't want it traced back to me."

"I'll see it's not," said Bill, "I just want you to deliver it to an old caravan on the edge of town, and don't worry about cost." He then pulled out a wad of notes and gave them to his old comrade. Chalkie did another silent whistle and said, "You always were a bit dangerous Billy Boy!"

"There's more if you need it," said Bill, "And I want a detonator that works off a radio signal."

"Is that all?" asked a bemused Chalkie.

"Yes," said Bill, "Remember, you owe me one."

"I owe you my life Billy Boy," said Chalkie.

In October, Peter was allowed home for a few days, Vicki got Doris to sit with him, but after a morning when he dribbled on her, she made an excuse and left. Towards the end of the month Peter came home to stay.

A nurse made a visit each day to help Vicki dress him. The nurse washed him and did a few jobs that Vicki felt she wasn't quite prepared for. Because he was constantly 'there', she couldn't stay in the house and would wander round the garden in some movie, usually set in New York. Some afternoons she would bundle him into the car and take him to the caravan, where he would sit outside dribbling in his wheelchair and stare at the distant tower. One afternoon a rough old white van turned up and a young man jumped out and opened up the rear doors. "This is for Bill," he said.

Towards the end of the month, Bill spent a couple of evenings up at the landfill, he told Jessie he was preparing a nice surprise for her, but Jessie was suspicious, he had not bothered her in the bedroom department for a few weeks. By the first of November all was ready and Bill said he had a special treat for her on Bonfire Night. Bill asked Vicki to decorate the caravan with Christmas decorations and put fresh sheets on the bed, which she thought a little odd. On the evening of the fifth, Bill drove Jessie up to Abbey Wood, and parked his car a long way from the caravan.

"Why have they moved the caravan?" asked Jessie.

"It was Vicki," said Bill, "She thought it would be more romantic for us away from the road.

"When Jessie entered the caravan, she couldn't believe her eyes, everything was dripping in tinsel. "Wow!" she said, "What's all this?"

"Well," said Bill, "I want to ask you to marry me."

"I said I would in Spain! Replied Jessie, "What the hell's got into you?"

"Ah, but it's different now, you see when we went to Scarborough I dropped into the estate agents and I've got some bungalows to show you, we could live there together, we don't have to get married if you want to be a free agent."

"But what are all the decorations about?"

"I wanted to make it special, I wanted to make it Bonfire Night and Christmas all at the same time, later we can cuddle up and listen to Matt Monroe on my old cassette player."

"Wow!" said Jessie.

Bill went outside and lit a few fireworks for Jessie who was wrapped up in a shawl by the door. They had a few shots of Brandy to ward off the cold, Bill made sure that she had more than him. At five to eight he put on Matt Monroe and said I'm just going outside to see if all the fireworks have gone out. He walked over to the crane, made sure that nobody was around, then set the charges. Back in the caravan Jessie had climbed into bed. After the brandy she found that it was quite warm under the duvet and she had stripped off most of her clothing. Bill stripped off and jumped into bed just as Matt was singing 'My Kind Of Girl'. "Oh Bill!" cried Jessie, "I love you!"

"Just a minute," said Bill and he grabbed a small device from the bedside chair.

"What are you doing?" asked Jessie.

"You'll see," said Bill as he punched a few keys, he then pressed 'send'.

Instantaneously, there was a huge explosion, the tower crane fell in a thousand pieces.   As the landfill erupted a huge crater was formed and for a short time an orange sky lit up the town. At the same time the old caravan was lifted into the air, Jessie looked up and saw a million bright stars as the roof blew off. Then the caravan fell over onto its side.

Bill fell onto Jessie and started huffing and puffing like an old, but perfectly tuned steam engine. "WOW!" cried Jessie in delight, "Wherever did you learn to do that?"

"In the Army," said Bill.

CHAPTER NINETEEN

"CONFESSIONS"

Within ten minutes the first fire engine had arrived followed by many more over the next hour. The police were quickly on the scene, along with a couple of ambulances and a helicopter. By midnight there were over fifty people attending. Angela was at a 'Meat and Potato Pie Festival' in Huddersfield. She drove straight there, quickly taking control of the situation. It was assumed that there were no casualties, but then an ambulance man relieving himself near the caravan, heard moaning noises and raised the alarm. A short ladder was brought over and to everybody's surprise, Bill and Jessie appeared together through the now horizontal door, rather like a captain of a submarine and his first mate, coming up for air after penetrating deep into the ocean. They both seemed a little light-headed, and when Bill was asked what he was doing up there, he replied, "Having a party!" Jessie said, "Merry Christmas, Ho! Ho! Ho!"

Vicki heard the bang, ran out into the garden and studied the western sky. Peter became very agitated, especially when she told him that the crane had gone and the whole of Abbey Wood was on fire. Angela called and told her about Bill and Jessie, who had been taken to the hospital for a check up. "I know this is nothing to do with you," she said, "But I want you to stay indoors, I'll call you tomorrow morning."

"Ok Chief," said Vicki, "But there's one thing you might do for me, can you get on to the hospital and see if they can take Peter? I think he's having some sort of fit, he's been very upset since I told him the news."

"I'm not surprised!" said Angela, "Now stay indoors, don't talk to the press, and wait for my call."

Peter was taken off to hospital in the middle of the night muttering his slurred version of 'Regeneration' and something that sounded like "I want to kill the bitch." At dawn, Vicki was woken by the phone, it was Angela, "Hi Angie," said Vicki, "Can I go out of the house yet?"

"Look out of your lounge window," said Angela. Vicki opened the curtains and was amazed to see around twenty people sitting in fold up chairs on her front lawn. There were more people, some with large cameras, out in the road, along with some big vans, with satellite dishes on their roofs.

"Oh my God!" cried Vicki, "What do they want with me?"

"Nothing!" replied Angela, "They want your old man, it's a good job we got him into the hospital last night! Now look here, whatever you do, don't talk to them, there's going to be a press conference at the town hall tomorrow morning, I want you there, we'll send a car."

"They are all staring at me," said Vicki.

"Well pull the curtains shut, don't answer the door or the telephone, and tomorrow, act stupid," said the Inspector, "They want someone to blame!"

Angela had advised Bill and Jessie to 'take a short holiday' until the dust had settled. Tom had disappeared and because the gutless John Pender and the rest of the

112

Council were laying low, all the old hacks had descended on Vicki's house. By mid morning it had started to rain and this helped to dampen the fire, which the Brigade had decided to leave until they had a better idea of what they were dealing with. Vicki opened the front door and was greeted with a firework display of flash bulbs. Everyone was talking at once, so she shut the door and went to Jamie's old room, where she found a trumpet which he had once played in the school band.

Armed with this instrument she went back, opened the door, and before they could restart their rampage, blew a long, loud note which seemed to have a stun gun effect on the rabble. "Right," she said in PMT mode, "I can't answer any questions until tomorrow, however you may all come in the dry and have a nice cup of tea."

"How about some cake?" said one hardboiled old crone at the back, "Perhaps you would help me to bake some?" shot Vicki, much to the amusement of the snake that was now pushing it's way into the hall and spilling out into every corner of the house.

After ten minutes of bedlam the media settled down, the queue for the bathroom subsided and even the old crone was helping with the refreshments. Vicki studied this motley bunch. They were all shapes and sizes, mostly shabby and pig ugly. Some of the women were giving a rather good impression of Mr. Punch while others smelt like Judy, but she reckoned they were just doing their job and she desperately needed them on her side. When they started to run out of supplies, a guy from the Times drove his car to the supermarket. Tracy, a young lady who usually did fillers on nutrition for a Sunday supplement, took charge of the cooking, along with a fat boy from one of the Red Tops. By midday the atmosphere was becoming very relaxed in a haze of cigarette smoke when a rather large young lady opened the front door and called out "Mum!" Vicki ran up and hugged her, "Linda!" she cried, "What the hell are you doing here!" From nowhere, each hack, young and old, produced a pen and notepad. "Excuse me boys and girls," shouted Vicki, "This is my daughter, well all right daughter in law, I will now request a press blackout for five minutes, we will be in my office!"

Vicki steered Linda into the bathroom and locked the door. She then started to inspect the floor and ceiling. "What are you looking for?" asked Linda.

"Bugs," replied Vicki.

"Look Mum," said Linda, "I saw the late news and I've come to make sure that you are alright, also I have three things to tell you, Jamie's been promoted, I've given up work, and we are going to have a baby next year."

"That's wonderful!" said Vicki, "But where's Jamie? its been so long since I've seen him and he should visit his father in hospital, why didn't he come with you?"

"He's on a seminar in Inverness," said Linda, "Getting motivated to supply 'quality management' in a 'hands on format' that may encourage interaction over a broad spectrum of the logistical playing field to suit the needs of the end user in a diverse spectrum."

"That's bullshit!" said Vicki, "He should be here, I don't know why he hates his father, but it's time we found out!" Vicki stormed into the Hall and grabbed the phone, "Give me his number," she said. Linda fumbled in her handbag for a piece of paper. "Here it is," she said "The

Transit Conference Hotel, Inverness." Vicki grabbed the piece of paper and keyed in the number.

An east European answered in that silly sing song voice that only people who go on 'Training Days' use. "I would like to speak to Mr Smith of North West Castings please," said Vicki.

"Zat is not pooossible," said the voice, "Eee is in conference at za moment!"

"Well you tell him to get to the phone right now!" roared Vicki in overdrive, "Tell him his father is dead and half the town has blown up, and if you can't do that, then put the Line Manager on the line pronto!"

"I val tell im," said a muted voice, "I val tell im to come, oo is Ponto?"

Five minutes later Jamie's voice came on the line, "Mum?" he said, "Are you alright?"

"What the hell are you playing at!" shouted Vicki, "I need you here and I need you now!"

"Mum," said Jamie, close to tears, "What's happened? Are you alright? I'm sorry about Dad, when he had his stroke, I wanted to visit, but it's difficult, I'll leave now, will arrive early tomorrow."

Vicki, who had calmed down, squeezed Linda's hand, and said quietly, "You Dad's not dead, but he might as well be, just come home love, just come home." When she looked up, the reporters were all scribbling away, she clapped her hands and in the silence that followed said, "Now that you are my friends, tomorrow at the news conference I will give you a statement, it will be important, I want you to make sure it goes global."

Jamie arrived at four am, a lone photographer at the

115

gate took a shot of his BMW, did a silent whistle and said "Nice car!" Linda was fast asleep in the spare bedroom, while Vicki sat in a chair by the door. After a big hug, Vicki asked, "I need to know why you hate your Dad, did he do something to you when you were a kid?" Jamie broke down and sobbed, then he said "It's not what you think Mum, ok I did find him in your bed with a woman a couple of times, but it's silly really, it's just that one day he found me looking in an open drawer in that little office of his under the stairs. I was looking for a pen and I found some money, a lot of money. I was about ten, and to a little boy it was fascinating, I was not going to take any of it, I was just counting it, looking at the pictures on the notes. Well, Dad went mad and he punched me with such force that I hit my head on the corner of the desk, I still have the scar. I was frightened to tell you in case he hit you. I think I told you that I did it playing football. Well ever since that day, he ceased to be my father, sorry, I can't forgive, but I will visit him in hospital."

"That's all I needed to know," said Vicki, "And if it makes you feel better, I can't forgive him either."

The Town Hall was filled to bursting point when Angela opened the press conference. She sat behind a long heavy table on a temporary stage hastily constructed at one end of the 'Great Hall'.

To her left was a young police officer in a smart new uniform and on her right sat Vicki. Her face had come out in large scarlet stars for the occasion. The fourth person, who sat a good distance to Vicki's right, was John Pender, wearing a regimental tie, and looking like a kangaroo with piles. The ladies, gentlemen and 'in-betweens' of the press took up the first eight rows, they were strangely quiet as they munched on goodies from their goody bags. These had been provided by Vicki and Linda. The townspeople filled the rest of the Hall, and they too were a little subdued, mainly by the outlandish Victorian architecture, as most had never set foot inside the building before.

Angela turned to the young policeman and they both nodded. The young man stood up and leaned towards a microphone, tapped it a couple of times, and said in a posh voice, "One, two, Your Worship the Deputy Mayor, Councillor John Tobias, Reginald Pender OBE, ladies and gentlemen of the press, residents of Liddingdale in the new regional district of North Moorland, I declare this press conference, concerning the recent events occurring at Abbey Wood, open. Inspector Angela Sadler of the North Moorland Police Authority, who is in charge of the Liddingdale Division, will read out a prepared statement, after which, you may ask questions, but I must warn you that the investigations are 'on going' and it is early days, we do not have all the answers yet and we (he looked at Angela) will not be drawn into supposition!" He sat down awkwardly with a pained expression as if his new uniform might have been a bit tight. "Get on with it!" said the old crone. Angela stood up wishing she had grown a little bit taller than her five foot ten. She turned over a few papers on the table and brought out an A4 lined refill pad. Vicki noticed that the handwriting was immaculate.

Angela spoke in a flat controlled voice, "Your Worship, Ladies and Gentlemen, here is the statement for the press prepared by the North Moorland Police, please do not interrupt, I will try my best to answer your questions later, but as my colleague has stated, the investigation is 'on going' at this point in time."

"Just say now!" said a rasping voice, "And get on with it!"

"Here is the prepared statement," said Angela as she put on a pair of 'Will Hay' pince-nez.

"On the evening of November 5th at approximately twenty hundred hours a large explosion, followed by a widespread fire, took place on a former 'landfill site' at Abbey Wood, an open area which lies two miles to the west of Liddingdale town centre. We (the Police) believe the explosion was caused by a stray firework landing on the site. We believe this, or some other external source ignited gas which had been seeping out of the ground. We do not at this stage believe that the explosion and fire were due to any foul play or suspicious circumstances. We are however building up a case against 'Smith's Recycling Ltd.' who we believe have been dumping unknown substances at the site over a number of years. This company has closed down. The Chief Executive, Mr. Peter Smith is unable to give us an interview at this time, due to having experienced a stroke. Most of the board members appear to be members of Liddingdale Borough Council. We (the Police) have asked Councillor Pender to represent them here today. Mrs Victoria Smith, wife of Mr. Peter Smith has no knowledge of the workings of the company and was not a board member or a shareholder. She was involved in a previous explosion at the site in June, when she received injuries to her face. After this earlier explosion, the Police were assured by the Council and Fire Service that the site was safe."

The young policeman stood up and said "Ladies and Gentlemen, you may now ask questions."

To everyone's surprise nothing happened for a few

seconds, then a slim young lady, who looked like a boy, stood up holding a thick wad of papers. As though talking to a jury, she said, loud and clear, "Inspector Sadler, my colleagues have asked me to be their spokesperson, I have all the relevant questions here. Vicki, er sorry Mrs Smith, thought it might be nicer and more grown up if we did it this way, my name is Pattie Parbold and I work for 'Single Women's Monthly (known in the trade as the 'Curse') I hope this is appropriate."

Angela looked in disbelief at Vicki, who looked back and smiled. Oh my God, thought Angela, My life is going down the toilet!

"My first question," continued Pattie with a satisfied look on her face, "Is one of my own which was not foreseen before we arrived, but one which we would all like to know the answer to, Where is the Fire Chief who confirmed back in June, that the Abbey Wood site was safe?"

The young officer made to get up but Angela rose to her feet, pushing him down like a can of peas in a shopping basket. She stood up and said, "Mr. Thomas McBean is unavailable at this point in time, his wife thinks he has gone off on a fishing trip, we have no forwarding address and his phone is dead, we have no reason at this time to think that his disappearance is suspicious, however we will be interviewing him when he gets back!"

"If he gets back!" said Pattie to laughter and applause from the auditorium.

"Nasty little cow," said Angela under her breath.

"I now turn to Mr. John Pender OBE," said Pattie in a sarcastic tone, "Can you produce a copy of the report on

119

Abbey Wood that sanctioned further building on the site after the demise of the bowling green, and can we know the names of the so called experts and consultants involved?"

John Pender coughed a number of times and asked Vicki to pass over a microphone.

"This summer," he said, "Liddingdale Borough Council have installed, for the benefit of our council tax payers, a brand new computer system (more laughs from the audience) and we are having teething problems with the software. We await the recovery of our ex Mayor, Mr Peter Smith who had access to the relevant documents and who was in charge of the project."

"Do you mean to say that you have lost all the records that a team of experts prepared for you at a cost of, and I quote, £20000?" snorted a now much bigger, but still flat chested, Pattie.

John sat there shaking his head, "I don't see the point of you being here," said Pattie.

"Well said Paddy!" croaked an old toad in an ancient brown suit, from the front row.

Pattie then turned to Angela and asked, "Can you tell us Inspector what the position of the Police is in this whole affair?"

Angela stood up and replied, "We were given to understand by the Council that the site was safe and I have copies here of a letter from the Fire Chief to say that the site presented no hazards to the general public. As it was surrounded by an eight foot high security fence, I was happy with the status quo.

"Ah!" said Pattie, throwing down her pile of paper,

much to the horror of the muckrakers in the third row, "But you weren't happy with the status quo were you? Because you have started an investigation up at the scrapyard, what made you do that?"

"That is a Police matter and is 'on going'" replied the Inspector, "I am not prepared to discuss this matter as it may affect future developments."

Pattie picked up the papers and neatly filed them, looking at Angela the whole time.

At this point, Vicki jumped up and said "I'll tell you why Inspector Sadler was investigating the dodgy goings on at Smiths Recycling, it's because she felt sorry for me."

To a hall of silent stunned faces, she continued, "Angela saved my life, she pulled me from the river the night that the Council planned to cut the heart out of Liddingdale! What did I have to live for? My husband, the Mayor, had ruined my face, he had forgotten my birthday and now he wanted, along with his cronies, to ruin our town!" She glanced at John, who now was planning a retirement in Weston-super-Mare at a home for damaged marsupials, his OBE now standing for 'One's Balls Exposed.' "She wanted justice, she's a good woman and a good cop, she's my Guardian Angel!" Angela tried to get Vicki back in her seat and only succeeded by saying, "You can have your say later!" Everybody cheered and some old hacks even shed a tiny tear from ducts that had been unused for decades, even the old crone said softly, "She's a lovely girl."

Pattie now turned on Angela in 'Ace Reporter' mode and struck the killer blow, ignoring the wishes of her comrades and sailing far into uncharted waters. "Tell me," she asked "How long were you, and Mrs Smith's husband, lovers?" To a hushed hall, Angela replied in a strong matter of fact voice, "About a year on and off."

"Perhaps more on than off?" enquired Pattie, without realising that she was getting a bit too clever.

Angela stood up and gave Pattie an icy stare, like a grown up would give to a naughty child, "I'm not perfect, in fact I've slept with quite a few married men, including a few high up coppers according to some people." She looked down on the reporter from the News of the World, and then continued, "I was taken in by Peter, like half the women in this town, he was handsome and charming, I was in love with him. We spent weekends in Paris, sorry Vicki I tried to spare you that, and he bought me expensive presents."

There was another lull in proceedings while everybody absorbed this new information. Pattie was now out of her depth and starting to lose the plot, along with her job, "So would you say it was a steamy affair?" she asked.

"Depends what you call steamy?" replied Angela, "As I doubt that you have ever had an affair with a man, you probably have no idea what's steamy and what's not!" Vicki started to get out of her seat again and Angela calmly walked over and changed places, "Just give me a couple of minutes more Tiger," she whispered. Angela grabbed hold of Vicki's microphone and walked to the front of the stage as if to break into song. "In a moment," she breathed, reducing every man there into non drip emulsion. "In a moment," she repeated, "My good friend Victoria Smith will talk to you, she is going to tell you about the future of our town, she will not dwell in the past. Don't you think it was unusual that she was not part of the company? That she was not included in the finances? She was the little wife who stayed at home, looked after the kids and did the washing. She cleaned the toilet and repaired the shed, she created a beautiful home and a fantastic garden, she was happy doing that and what did she get in return? She got a face, that's what she got. A face with bloody stars on it!"

After another theatrical pause she continued, "All I wanted was promotion, I was the best Constable of my year, within a short time I was promoted, and yes I slept with a few people and I lost a child in the process." She looked at Pattie as a giant looks down on some long dead insect, "Yes I made mistakes lots of them, but I was, and still am the best copper Liddingdale ever had!" This last statement received great applause, she went on, "I have applied for an inner city job that involves promotion, but now, after this briefing, I will withdraw my application. I may be forced by the likes of Mr.Pender and his friends in high places, to resign, and unlike them I wont get an OBE from the Queen for doing sod all!"

A deathly hush permeated the building seeping into the very fabric from floor to ceiling.

After another strategic pause Angela threw down the microphone and jumped off the stage, she walked to the centre of the hall and said in a strong clear voice, "For the time being I remain in charge here and I want to stay if you will have me, even if I end up as a glorified lollipop lady!" She turned and walked out, ran down the steps to the road and jumped into the nearest police car. "Take me home Phil," she said, "I've had enough of the media circus for one morning."

CHAPTER TWENTY

"PARADISE POSTPONED"

After Angela left the hall, all eyes turned to Vicki. She was just about to speak when John Pender stood up, and with much scuffing and scraping of chairs, extricated himself from the table.   He walked briskly behind Vicki and the young policeman, dropped down the three temporary steps, and made for the door. The first one he tried was a fire exit, but the bar was stuck, so he ran down the side of the hall to the grand entrance, a beautiful pair of panelled oak doors under a gothic arch. He pushed one of the large brass handles, and as the door silently opened, a single voice cried out, "Judas!"

Some of the townspeople made to follow, but the old crone suddenly appeared by the doors and stopped them. She gave them the 'evil eye', which was her normal look, and said in a rasping voice, "You will stay!" All eyes once again turned to the stage where a small woman with a funny red face stood fumbling with a school exercise book. She put the book down on the table, cleared her throat and said, "Before I start I want to tell you that Angela, that is Inspector Sadler, was being kind when she said that I was the 'Good Little Wife'. I may not have received the expensive presents some of the other women got, but I had my son, my house and my garden. I knew things were not right but I turned a blind eye because I hoped that one day he would change. Now I will lose the lot, but at least I can start again, by leaving me out of the business he did me a favour. I knew something was wrong down at the Council, but what could I do? The man who is responsible for all of this, including my face, is not here and neither is his partner in crime Harry Bains!"

A gasp went around the hall as Vicki continued, "I remember a conversation between Peter and Harry about a report on Abbey Wood that said the land would not be stable for at least one hundred years, and as to consultants and experts, where do you think most of that £20000 went?" Vicki walked to the far end of the table and picked up a large parcel wrapped in brown paper, walked back, gave it to the young officer and said, "This will take Harry and half of the Council out of circulation for a while, I smashed open Peter's bureau last night, it's not everything, he carried a lot in his head, but it's enough." She patted the young man on the head and said, "You can go Paul, what I have to say now has nothing to do with recent events." Paul went to get up but changed his mind and said, "I think I'll stay, there's a little old woman with a bit of 4 by 2 guarding the door!"

Vicki picked up the exercise book and said, "Ladies and Gentlemen of the Press, first of all I must tell you that I started the fire by blowing up that rusty old crane! I went up there with some very big fireworks and a box of matches, and when nobody was looking, I blew it to kingdom come!" At this point the whole audience burst into laughter. "But to be serious," Vicki continued, "All the time my husband was planning to build his monstrosity at Abbey Wood, I was planning to build a beautiful park on the site. I wanted to restore the land, make it well again.

I had wonderful ideas and dreams of a huge open park on the lines of Central Park, New York. There would be wide avenues, lakes and ponds. There would be tea shops and bars, thousands of trees and gardens, lots of them. There would be a Japanese Garden and an Indian Garden, a New Zealand Garden and a meadow, a huge wild flower meadow stretching as far as the eye could see. The people of Liddingdale could go to the park on Sundays and have picnics, folk would visit from all over the world, and in one corner of the park I would build a small factory that would produce genuine Liddingdale glass again. In the centre there would be a glass tower that caught the sun."

Vicki stopped to sip water from a glass. She looked down on the reporters. They were hard, worldly, and cynical. They all hoped an orphanage might burn down at any moment to provide them with a good story. But there they sat, wide eyed and spellbound like kids at a Saturday morning picture show. She looked towards the door, the old crone was dabbing her one eye with a filthy handkerchief. Vicki threw the book down, walked to the front of the stage, and sat on the table. "My friends," she said, "My lovely new friends from the great information gathering highway. When I nearly died I saw Eden and I wanted to go through the door and smell the flowers, but I couldn't because I knew I had to build my garden here in Liddingdale. The one thing I did not consider was how much it would cost. I thought people might contribute the money. I did not want committees, consultants, or charities creaming off their share. I did not want contractors or politicians charging the earth, like they do on those big Government projects that go way over budget, I did not want that top heavy, overblown European Union mucking it up like they muck up everything else! I did not want any greedy snouts in my trough! I was quite sure that the cash would come from like minded people, kindred spirits you might say. If there is a God somewhere, I thought he might also help me out a bit!"

Vicki got down off the table and walked to the centre of the stage, "Before the explosion," she said, "I was hoping that the landfill would support Elysium, I knew they could never put a large heavy building up there, but I thought most of the gas may have seeped away. Now we have a huge hole in the ground and the rest is still on fire, and could be on fire for days, weeks, even years!" She looked down towards the press and continued, "What I want you to do for me is find somebody, anybody, even if you have to go to the ends of the earth. I want you to find somebody to help me."

Our town is here because of the sand that came from that place, I have to put something back, it may not be the Elysian Fields but it will be our Eden!" Vicki waved to the old crone and said in a kindly voice, "It's alright Roberta, you can let them go home now." Paul and Vicki stepped down off the stage to a standing ovation.

During the next half hour there was much kissing and shaking of hands. One or two of the more human ones even did little hugs in the less public parts of the hall. Jane, a hard bitten old hack from a down market scandal sheet, pressed a grubby card in Vicki's hand, and said, "There's always a place for you in Potters Bar." Ed Sturgen from 'Far North Television' whispered in Vicki's ear, "I need you on Sunday in our Carlisle studio for the 'Let's go

Green!' programme, we are giving it over to a phone-in with a visual link up to Chicago, I'll send a limo." Three reporters, from the Sunday Billet, the Times and the Daily Star, drew lots for the rights to Vicki's life story. The Lady from the Sunday Billet won and asked Vicki to go down to London for a few days.

Vicki walked out into the sunshine her head spinning, Liddingdale had never looked better.

A large silver car drew up, it was Jamie. As they drove home he said, "I'm sorry about your face Mum, I didn't know what to say."

"You should have seen it five months ago!" said Vicki.

Jamie pulled the car off the road and stopped, "Look Mum," he said, "I'm so sorry, I've been wrapped up in work , we need the money. I'm sorry, I've not been a very good son, I should have tried harder, I wanted to."

"I was a crap daughter," said Vicki, "None of us are what we want to be, life is not a movie or a play, we just have to muddle through it the best we can."

When they arrived at the house Linda told Vicki that there had been two phone calls, one from Jessie and one from Allan. The autumn sun turned the garden into a print from Selfridges.

Linda asked, "Who's this Allan?"

"Oh just one of my boyfriends!" said Vicki.

"Not anymore," replied Linda, "He asked me to tell you that Monica is fine and that he has met a young lady at college, and yes, she is a proper woman, he's done all the usual checks."

"What did Jessie want?" asked Vicki, quickly changing the subject.

"Am I a proper woman?" Linda suddenly asked Jamie.

"Well if you're not," said Jamie, "When you've had the baby we can join a circus!"

"Jessie," said Linda, "Wants you to call her, the number's by the phone, some bed and breakfast place on the East Coast."

Vicki called Jessie but Bill answered, "Thanks Dad," she said, "Thanks for everything, are you ok? I hear you had a close shave."

"I'm fine lass," said Bill, "Perhaps it would be best if we didn't mention the subject again?"

"Ok Dad," said Vicki, "I want to ask a favour but it's got nothing to do with that."

"I'm very glad to hear it!" said Bill.

"When you see the papers tomorrow there will be quite a lot about me in them, I will be away in London for a week or maybe longer. I am going to get some money for my life story so I think I will be allright financially after they take the house back."

"You have Edith's bungalow, that's yours lass!" said Bill, "You are my little girl now remember."

"That's so very kind of you Dad," said Vicki, "I would like to move some of my personal items there, like my clothes and Aunty Betty's old sewing machine, if that's all right?"

Linda and Jamie stayed on until Sunday when a stretched limo whisked Vicki off to Carlisle. Jessie had phoned back, and Vicki told her what had happened in the town since the explosion.

Jessie said that they had made an offer for an old cottage near Flamborough and they were getting married after Christmas. Jessie asked Vicki, if she had ever had an orgasm? Vicki was a bit surprised at this question and asked what happened in the caravan. "Oh," said Jessie, "There was a big bang and the next thing I knew, Bill was on top of me."

"What happened then?" asked Vicki.

"Ho! Ho! Ho!" replied Jessie.

CHAPTER TWENTY ONE

"CARLISLE"

The Far North Television Studio in Carlisle was an old railway shed. Some interior designer had done her best with it, but it was still an old railway shed. Far North was in financial difficulties finding life harsh in the multi-media world of the twenty first century. It made a reasonable job of covering local news, and like most of its kind, was obsessed with sport. The jewel in its box was Percy Green. Here was a guy who lived for the environment, the 'King of the Compost Heap'. If ever someone was in the right place at the right time, and had the right name, it was Percy. He had started his career in local newspapers and gravitated to radio in his native Scotland. When an opening came up to do a half hour gardening slot each week on 'Far North', he got the job. The programme (Percy's Patch) became extremely popular with neglected spinsters, mainly due to Percy's good looks, rugged charm and ill fitting trousers. Within a year, Percy had moved his whole family down from Stirling. After two years, 'Far North' gave him an extra programme on Sunday evening to compete with the BBC. The new programme, on green issues, was an instant success. Repeats were shown on cable channels world wide. It was especially popular in the USA.

Vicki was overwhelmed and a little pensive. The programme went out live at eight in the evening. She was sitting in a converted coal stage, known optimistically as 'The Green Room'. She tried to read a couple of tired magazines, but she was nervous, the stars on her face had become ugly triangles, she wanted to go home.

Around two o' clock Percy burst into the room, shook Vicki's right hand until it hurt, and like a clown at a child's party, bounced up and down with enthusiasm. He rattled off the schedule for the evening's programme in a thick lilting accent. He grabbed a chair and sat down opposite Vicki, he could see she was shaking. "Don't worry," he said, "It's only television! Live television tonight I grant you, but still only television!" He looked at her face, "Does it hurt?" he asked.   "Not anymore," replied Vicky, who was now crying. "There, there," said Percy, who covered both of her hands with his. She noticed how big and warm they were. She looked up into his face, it was a kind face. "Let me tell you something," he said, "This will be my first time live, I'm flying without a parachute, if this lot goes plop plop, it's the job centre for me!" Vicki started to feel better, "They want to change my face," she said.

"Who wants to change your face?" asked Percy.

"Make up," said Vicki.

Percy stood up, he must have been well over six foot, "And do you want to change your face?" he asked, in a way that reminded Vicki of a priest extracting a confession.

"No!" she shouted, "Not for some poxy television show!"

"That's the spirit!" said Percy, "You are going to be great tonight! Come on, let's get out of here, we have a wonderful cathedral in Carlisle, I'll give you a tour, and by the way, my real name's Bob, Bob Bassett." Vicki and Bob had a great afternoon looking round the city. Over tea they discussed the way they would interact in the studio and how they would handle each issue as it arose. He was particularly looking forward to the 'phone in' section. A new dawn had arrived at 'Far North Television!

Vicki was in a pretty green dress, which they said she could keep, she looked almost normal.

The introductory music was played and the captions came up on the monitors. A 'warm up man' subdued the small over excited audience with elaborate hand gestures, as the floor manager counted Percy in, "four, three, two, one!"

"Good evening," said Percy, looking like everybody's favourite uncle, "A warm welcome from the city of Carlisle, here in the beautiful Borders, between the Southern Uplands and the Eden Valley. Tonight's extended programme is unique, because as our guest we have a very special lady, a lady on a mission, a lady who said, and I quote (at this point he put on a pair of expensive looking spectacles and picked up a clip board) 'I want to make the earth well again!' Sitting here beside me is Victoria Smith a lady who wants to build Elysium!" The audience, whipped into frenzy, erupted in manic applause. Vicki glanced across at Percy, he looked back and winked, they were in complete control of the Star Ship.

On the monitors were pictures of Liddingdale spliced in with news footage of the fire, there was even film of Vicki giving her speech in the town hall. This went on for around five minutes and ended with the audience applauding once again. The floor manager pointed to Percy, who looked at a camera, and said "Tonight we are linked to the world, we will be visiting a number of countries in this special extended programme. For the second half of our programme we will be talking live to Professor Gary Pickering of Lakeside University, Chicago. He is an expert on green issues."

Another bloody expert, thought Vicki.

They then went to a commercial break, a young girl mopped Percy's brow but kept well clear of Vicki, who felt that perhaps she should wear a bell around her neck.

The following section of the programme concentrated on the global link and visited a number of countries where environmental concerns were discussed. After another break, there was a fifteen minute phone in from the UK. Percy showed his skill in dealing with callers, learned the hard way in local radio with its fixation over hours of bland music for Baby Boomers. He knew just how to cut people off in mid-rant without being rude or causing offence.

For the second hour of the show they went live to Chicago, Percy made a big thing of this and the audience responded like inmates given too many sweets in a home for the insane. The professor looked just as Vicki imagined he might, mid sixties with long untidy grey hair. His unkempt appearance was supported by an ancient pair of glasses that needed constant attention. Behind these lived a pair of brilliant blue eyes. His face resembled an old sack of potatoes left by the roadside and he wore an ill fitting sports jacket with non matching tie. So much for the land of plenty, thought Vicki. Behind the professor was a picture of the Lake Shore Towers against a cloudless sky. "Good evening Professor Pickering," said Percy. "Good afternoon," said the professor, with a smile that made his eyes sparkle, as he fought a losing battle to keep his glasses on.

"I would like to introduce you to Vicki," said Percy, "Have you been watching the show so far?"

"Indeed I have," said the professor, "Oh hi Vicki, yes I have been following your progress over the last few days with great interest and I will be pleased to answer any questions on landfill, but I must warn you, it's not an exact science. "May I call you Gary?" asked Percy, oozing with as much charm as a person from Stirling can muster. "Sure can Percy!" said Gary with a smile.

Vicki, now in full control, went straight off on a tangent and asked, "Does your family come from Yorkshire by any chance?"

"Why do you ask?" replied a smiling Gary. "Because I think it's a Yorkshire name," said Vicki.

"Well, maybe they do, way back, but I'm a New York Pickering, the name comes from the Pickerings of New York!"

"Great!" said Vicki, "Have you been to Central Park? What's it like?"

"No," answered Gary, "Never been there."

This last remark started a conversation that had Percy looking up at the Director's cabin with the face of the boy who lost his parents when they moved to another town while he was at school.   Percy started to wonder where the job centre might be in Carlisle, if it might be open on Monday and if there were any jobs vacant on 'Radio Nowhere'?

"Why haven't you been there?" asked Vicki in a tone that might be used when scolding a child.

"Because you are talking about New York City," said

Gary, "And I'm from Owego, Up State New York! Let me explain, I'm from New York State, not New York City, Central Park's in Manhattan. New York City is not America just like Berlin is not Germany and London is not England!"

"Sorry," said Vicki, "Would you like to go and visit Central Park?"

"Sure would!" said Gary "I'll meet you at The Boathouse, like in the movies!"

"It's a date!" replied Vicki, "But I don't know when, I have my own park to build first, tell me about Owego, is it nice there."

"It is," said Gary, "I miss it, I once had a vacation in England went to London and Stratford, one place that reminded me of Up State was your beautiful Cotswold Hills, have you been there?"

"No," said Vicki.

"I think we need to get out more," said Gary.

They went into another commercial break, Percy made sure they were 'off air' and said to Gary, "Professor, I think we need to get back to the matter in hand, we are running out of time, this link up is expensive and could finish off Far North Television!"

When they went back on air, Vicki noticed a man step out of an upstairs office with a sheet of white card, on which was written "WELL DONE GANG, 10,000,000 WATCHING! VICKI WE LOVE YOU!"

This had an amazing effect on Percy, who became his brash, confident self again. Gary continued, "It is very difficult to give you an answer on this landfill site Vicki, because nobody is sure what's down there, and from what

I gather we will never know for certain, even to give an optimistic guess on when you could start once the fires are out, would be almost impossible."

"If it was not too bad, would you say around five years?" asked Vicki.

"More like fifty years," said Gary, "Look I know how much you want to do this, but these big sites are dangerous, I really would have to see it for myself before I could even hazard a guess."

The floor manager put two fingers up to Vicki, she turned to the big screen beside her and said to Gary, "Well thanks Professor, it's been great talking to you."

"The pleasure's been all mine," said Gary, "And by the way don't forget our date!"

"Can't wait," said Vicki. "The Big Apple will wonder what's hit it when the Owego Kid with the scary specs and the Liddingdale Lady with the funny face ride into town!"

CHAPTER TWENTY TWO

"THE IDEA"

Vicki got home just after midnight, there were some emails. The Sunday Billet mailed her, there was a return ticket waiting at the railway station. They had booked her on the 10.05 (change at Leeds) to London, where there would be a car to take her to a west end hotel, they reckoned it would take two or three days to ghost write her biography. The BBC needed her, and a couple of magazines wanted an interview. As she logged off, she realised this story had captured the public's imagination, there was no going back. There were also some messages on her phone, including two from the hospital asking when she could come and take Peter home, as his speech was returning and he was upsetting the other patients. There was a good luck message from Angela, who had watched the programme. She also said, before the machine ran out of tape, that they had found more evidence at the scrapyard, and in some of the papers that Vicki had provided. They now had a better idea of what was the *tip of a very large iceberg." (Pardon the pun!)

Vicki spent four nights in London, during which time she had her life story written, gave a number of interviews (with permission of the Sunday Billet) and did a little shopping. She also, for the first time in her life, opened her own bank account. The Daily Missive opened a special account to take the money that was now pouring in from all over the world. On TV, Vicki stressed that the money would be invested for the time being, as she might have to re-think her plans, due to the fire.

A couple of large Dutch companies had promised to supply plants, and an engineering firm in Kalamazoo wanted to build and run the glassworks.

Bert Bradshaw, the well known North Country comic and racing driver, would sponsor the central tower, if he could name it after his mother, Joyce, who's suet puddings were worshiped all over Bronte Land. All this worried Vicki, but something inside drove her on, she was an express train with no brakes, she was in control, but only as long as she kept on the level and all the signals were at green.

Vicki did not like London and was glad to get home. Bill picked her up from the station, he told her that their offer for the cottage had been accepted, and they would be moving in the New Year. Jessie had sold 'Bella Vista' to Debbie and Sharon, but would keep the flat as a 'bolthole' for when they came back to visit the town. Vicki told Bill that she would be able to stay in her house until after Christmas, but she needed to move her personal items to the bungalow. "I'll give you a hand," said Bill. "Accepted," said Vicki. "There's another thing," said Bill, "I haven't been up to Abbey Wood since the fire, they say it's almost out now, when we've finished bumping, shall we pay a visit or are you frightened of what you might see?"

"I am a bit scared Dad," said Vicki, "But yes we must go and look, I don't know what to do, but thousands of nice ordinary people believe in me, they want me to succeed, I must find an answer."

"You will," said Bill, "I believe that Enid waited for the right time to die, Jessie said I was needed to help somebody here, I believe that's you. Trouble is I don't know the answer either, but between us we'll come up with something."

Vicki spent Saturday sorting out her stuff, she called a man with a van to take the rest away leaving the basics, a bed, a chair, a table. She also hired a self drive van for the following Tuesday.

On Sunday they decided to spend a day at the bungalow. Angela was invited to what they called a 'Pre House Warming Party'.

Vicki liked the idea of living in this funny old place, slap bang in the town centre. She started drawing up plans in her head of what the garden might look like after the first year, it took her mind off the park in her darker moments. The hospital rang every day and Vicki decided to ask for another week of freedom, she told them she was moving house. Angela looked ten years younger, she was staying on for the time being and there had been some nice letters about her in the local papers. The investigation into 'Smith's Recycling' was going well and a good case against the Directors was being made. She didn't know if Peter would ever be brought to trial, although his condition was improving. Dave would probably be given a suspended sentence, if proved guilty, as he had been a great help to the Police. Vicki was glad about this, as he was married with six young children. On their own, in the tiny back garden, Vicki said, "Angie I have a grand in cash back at the house, I think it may be stolen."

"Forget it!" said Angela, "Don't muddy the water, stick it in that special account at the Sunday Billet, from Brenda Bloggs of Blogg Street, Bloggsville USA.

"But it's a lot of money!" protested Vicki.

"What money?" said Angela, as she went indoors for another flapjack.

On Monday, Vicki made a visit to the hospital. Peter was not pleased to see her. "I want to go home," he said in a disjointed way. "Next week," said Vicki, "And I'll fix up a nurse for you!"

"You can look after me!" said Peter, "You're my wife, and you promised to at our wedding remember?"

"And you promised to take me to New York!" replied Vicki.

"I could spill the beans, and where would that leave your new friend Angela?" said Peter, trying not to dribble on his new dressing gown.

"If you say anything about Angie your bones will be crushed by twenty five tons of Pennine rock," said Vicki in a cold detached voice, "And by the way, did you know that your friend Harry Bains has been arrested? He got as far as Huddersfield apparently, and then there's your old mate Tom McBean, he's up in Falkirk where he walked in front of a train, they've found most of him, just need a leg and a hand."

When she returned to the house, Vicki popped next door to see Doris, they had not spoken since the dribbling incident. After a long wait, Doris finally opened the door with the look of a woman who once found her husband wearing a dress. "Hi," said Vicki, "Just thought you'd like to know that Peter will be home soon, you can visit if you like."

"I'm too busy," said Doris, "I have my committees!"

"Well I thought I'd let you know that they are letting us stay here until after Christmas, I have a nice little place in Mill Street to move into next year."

"And what about your husband?" enquired Doris, "Is he going with you?"

"Well that depends if he's a good boy," said Vicki, "And of course if he recovers too much he may be moving to his own bedsit with a big lock on the door."

"He should be home! You should be looking after him!" said Doris, "Instead of gallivanting around the country talking about a stupid park that nobody wants!"

"You are so right!" said Vicki, "Well must go, people to see, lots to do, give my love to Hubbie and the boyfriend!"

Tuesday was a beautiful day, the Pennines stood tall, the sky was sapphire. Vicki left the house early and drove twenty miles south to a small village, where you could hire any sort of van you wanted, as long as it was white, rusty and had dents in it.

When she saw the van it was a little bigger than she had imagined it would be, but the nice young man said she would be ok with it because it had big mirrors. "Why do you call it a Luton Van," she asked, "Does it come from Luton?"

"Oh no!" the young lad laughed, "The first ones did, they carried straw hats, that's why it's got that bit over the cab, like a hat!"

Vicki thought this conversation was well on the way to

Central Palukaville, so she smiled, turned the key, and roared off up the Cattle Road. She picked up Bill at the flat, Jessie was helping in the salon. The recent publicity had brought a lot of people into town and the whole place had a busy feel to it. Liddingdale looked young, the town was dancing, playing games, wearing a party dress.

They managed to take all of Vicki's effects in one go, and after a quick tea break, Vicki drove Bill up to Abbey Wood in the van. There were a number of sightseers there and Bill noticed that the remains of the caravan had been taken away. There was even a motor coach, which had brought a WI from Bramble Hill on a day trip. They walked alongside the fence, which had been repaired. Vicki could not see any remains of the crane, that part of the area had been tidied up, but inside the fence there was debris everywhere, and where the crane had stood was a huge hole that had swallowed up part of the road. "You don't do anything by halves Dad!" whispered Vicki.

"Its strong stuff!" muttered Bill.

They walked right around the site in silence, the devastation was total. It was a wasteland. Everything was black, and here and there, smoke drifted lazily out of holes in the earth. After about twenty minutes, Bill said, "I am so, so sorry lass, I think I overdid it I wanted to destroy the crane!"

"You did that alright!" said Vicki.

Vicki sat down on the black earth and put her head in her hands. Bill turned away and looked out to the distant hills, "I should have blown the lot up," he said.

"That's it!" cried Vicki, "That's it, that's what we have to do. Oh Bill! You were sent here to tell me how to do it, that's it! Why didn't I think of it before? I should have blown the lot up, not just the crane, but the whole site, I know what to do!" With this, she did a sort of tribal dance, grabbed hold of Bill and pulled him down onto the ground. She found the remains of an old bucket and forced it onto his head, then sat down beside him and said, "This is going to be the best park in the universe!"

Bill thought it wise to remain still. He had never seen a woman go mad before. After what seemed a lifetime, Vicki said in a cool, calm voice, "We get the Army to come and blow the whole site up, a little bit here, a little bit there, not enough to make big holes, it's just the rubbish we want to 'free up', then we get some big earthmoving equipment, like bulldozers, to push all the rubbish to the middle, where we will create a small hill. Bill, who was listening intently, said "But this stuff will be going off for the next hundred years!"

"Yes," said Vicki, we need to vent off the gas, don't you see? We need a chimney in the middle of the pile, a great big chimney right in the middle we need a chimney, not a tower!"

"And what form will this chimney take?" asked Bill.

"Well," said Vicki, "I will have to consult the Professor, but I can see a steel pipe full of holes, about ten feet across and as high as we like, sunk into the ground with three external legs, a bit like those flying buttresses on old churches. After the Army has done their work, it will be good training and publicity for them, we build the chimney, and cover it in pieces of glass, cut like diamonds, to catch the sun.

Bill, who was now getting quite interested, but was still

144

a little worried over his new daughter's sanity, suddenly said, "I don't want to rip your dream to shreds, but there are two major problems with all this."

"Fire away Daddy!" said a very calm and collected Vicki.

"Well first," said Bill, "You are going to push all this landfill, containing God knows what, up towards a chimney, it will surround the chimney like a cone, a cone that I estimate could be over fifty feet high and half a mile across! A hill of stinking manure! Secondly, at the front of the site, we have a big hole, what the hell are you going to do with that?"

"Easy peasey," said Vicki, as she did a little twirl, "We cover the pile in a membrane that breathes, I'm sure the Prof will come up with something, we might even be able to cover that with plants to absorb the smell. As the years pass, the pile will collapse in on itself rather like a star dropping into a bucket! Another added advantage for the park, is that people will travel far to see it, because it will be the biggest compost heap in the world!"

"Ok," said Bill, feeling a little out of his depth, "What about the crater, I suppose you are going to tell people that was caused by a meteorite?"

"Good thinking!" replied Vicki, "We will put a roof right across it. We will make it the grand entrance!"

"Ah," said Bill, "You are going to create a gigantic greenhouse, a whole rainforest?"

"Of course not! Don't be silly!" said Vicki.

"Well why do you need a roof?" asked Bill.

"Because," said Vicki, "Under the roof will be a glass factory, a restaurant and a shop."

CHAPTER TWENTY THREE

"CLOSING THE DOOR"

Vicki and Bill ran back to the van, like two kids let out of school early. An American woman came up and asked, "Are you the lady on TV?" Vicki hesitated for a moment, "Yes," she said.

"I just want you to know," said the lady, "That I think what you are doing here is great!"

"It's a mess!" cried out Vicki, "It's a bloody mess!"

"This place can be mended, you will make it better, I believe that there is a way," said the lady, "At this moment it is just a notion in somebody's head, the whole world's dying, build this park, it will be the first of many, you will find a way."

"I think I might have found a way," replied Vicki.

On the journey back to town, Bill said, "There's one thing that I don't understand."

"I thought that I explained it pretty well," said Vicki, "Sorry about the old bucket on your head, I got a bit carried away, can you take it off? We're getting funny looks!"

"That's ok," said Bill, "At least you didn't ask me to kick it! I want to be serious, look when you have pushed up this great pile of doggy doo dah, you'll be back to square one."

"I don't follow," said Vicki.

"Well," said Bill, "You will be left with a worked out

sand pit, the soil, what there is of it, is pretty rough, and you want to build a world class park."

Vicki stopped at the lights, controlling the traffic flow over the town bridge crossing the River Lid.

"It will be a long term thing," said Vicki, as she drove across the narrow bridge, "It will take months, maybe years to get permission to do anything up there, then at least a year to push up the heap and build the chimney. My idea is that it should belong to the town."

"It already does," said Bill.

"No, what I mean," said Vicki, "Is that everyone who lives here will have a share, and everyone will be able to take part in creating the park, adding bits here and there."

"That would be chaos!" cried Bill.

"Nature is chaos, life is chaos!" Vicki replied, "And anyway, I'll be in charge!"

Bill, who had been lost in thought, looked up, and with alarm said, "Where are you taking me? We're driving out of town."

"I have to top up the tank, before I take Lulu back," said Vicki.

"Do you have to call a tatty old white van Lulu?"

"Of course I do, I can see you there Dad, in a boater at a jaunty angle just like Maurice Chevalier! You'd have all the girls in Luton running after you!"

"I don't think I will ever understand women," sighed Bill.

Vicki stopped at a petrol station, and when she returned, Bill noticed that she had been shopping. She dumped a couple of bags on the seat between them and carefully placed a bunch of flowers on Bill's lap. They drove on in silence for a short distance and stopped on a long lay-by outside the town cemetery. The original part of the cemetery was away to the right on the other side of the road, while to the left was the overspill surrounding a new crematorium that looked like a church with an extra large belfry to let the smoke out.

Vicki picked up the flowers, opened the door and walked across the road, Bill followed. In an undisturbed corner, she brushed some coarse grass away to reveal a small head stone.

"My Dad," she said.

"I shouldn't be here," said Bill, "This is a private moment."

"He wouldn't mind," said Vicki softly, "He would be glad that you are here, looking out for me. He was a lovely person."

Vicki put the flowers down on the grave and started to cry, "What is it?" Bill asked.

"I was a lousy Daughter," said Vicki, "Cold as ice, I loved him, but he never knew."

"That's not true and you know it!" said Bill.

"But I never told him, don't you understand? I never told him and now it's too late! I haven't been here for years."

"I'm sure he knew," said Bill.

"But why am I like this?" asked Vicki, "Why can't I show emotion like other people?"

"I think you are doing a pretty good job now," said Bill, "Life is not perfect, life is not 'Happy Families', life is real, life is tough."

Vicki took a small bag from her coat pocket, from this

she produced a toy sports car which she placed on the grave under the head stone, "Jessie tells me you're a poet," she said.

She took a small piece of card from her pocket and said "Read this."

"What is it?" he asked, turning the card over in his hand.

"It's a poem for Dad," said Vicki, "Please read it, you see I have to close the door.

Bill fumbled for his glasses, then he walked over to the path, he wanted to give Vicki some time with her Dad. He looked down and read…

"I never said I loved you,
I never said I care,
I rarely said I'm sorry,
I was not always there,
And on the day they took you,
And put you in the ground,
I showed few signs of sorrow,
To the people gathered round,
But how the past now haunts me,
Dark shadows in my head,
The cross I have to carry,
Too many words unsaid."

Bill walked back and gave the poem to Vicki, she placed it under the sports car.

As they walked back towards the road, Bill asked, "Where's your mother buried?"

"I don't know," said Vicki, "She left when I was five."

"I'm sorry," said Bill.

"I feel a bit guilty over Jess," said Vicki, "I want to call her Mum, but I can't."

"Can I drive Lulu home?" asked Bill, like an overgrown schoolboy.

"Go on then Maurice!" said Vicki, with a smile.

CHAPTER TWENTY FOUR

"LOOSE ENDS"

When Vicki got home, she called Gary in Chicago. He was busy, but someone must have told him, as later in the day, he called back.

"Hi," he said, "Do I still have a date with a Funny Face?"

"Of course Owego!" said Vicki, "I've got something important that I want to discuss with you."

"Sorry Vicki," said Gary, "You are a lovely girl, but I can't marry you, been there, tried it, very, very, expensive!"

"How many times?" asked Vicki.

There was a long pause until Gary said in a reluctant tone, "Three, how about you?"

"Once," replied Vicki, "But that was enough!"

"So what are we going to talk about?" asked Gary.

"I think I have a plan worked out, but I need to chew it over with you, can we meet?"

"How about the Boathouse?"

"Great! but when? and how? Oh my God this is not happening! Do I need a visa?"

"Calm down, we'll sort it all out, 'Far North' have asked me to do a programme on Central Park next year, and that newspaper from London has been chasing me for my non existent sex life! They want to make up some sort of romantic thing about us, sort of happy ever after type fairy tale, we might as well play along and take the money while it's there!"

"Ok Owego, I'll leave the small print to you, we have a date, I'll be wearing a red and purple face and Gary, please do something for me."

"What's that?"

"Buy some new clothes, now that we are going to be film stars!"

"Ok Marilyn Monroe!"

"Bye Owego take care."

"You too Funny Face."

In the evening 'Far North' called and told her the 'date' would be in two weeks time, Gary had asked how long she would be staying in New York, as he wanted to take her 'Up State'.   "I'll think about it," she said, "But I don't want cameras following us around all the time."

"No problem," said the guy at 'Far North' "We want you to have some quality time alone, we need you to bond in a multi-functional way."

"Do you mean have sex?" asked Vicki.

"Sex would be good," said the guy.

The next day Vicki went to see Joe Willmott who was now head of the Council. He would never be Mayor as he did not believe in such trifles. Joe lived in a small terraced house near the River Lid, it had belonged to his Dad. Joe had been a highly skilled glass blower at 'Bensons' and was very interested in Vicki's plan to build a new glassworks in the town. He was not so sure about the glass tower (Vicki did not mention it would be a chimney) as he could only concentrate on one thing at a time. Vicki and Joe, along with his tiny wife Diddy, had a long discussion about the future of Abbey Wood, and when she left, Vicki felt that the Council and most of the population were with her all the way, holding her tight, sharing the dream, not letting her fall.

Back at Abbeyfield Drive, there was a message on the phone, it was from her local MP, he wanted Vicki to attend a meeting in London on Friday and give a talk to a "Regeneration Group." Vicki realised that he was trying to gain a few 'Brownie Points' for a tired and unpopular government, but decided to go and fight her corner. She was determined however not to get bogged down in organised politics and religion. They had done far too much damage in the past. Having a fake romance with Gary was one thing, it brought a bit of pleasure into humdrum lives, selling her soul to the Philistines was something else. It was not part of the dream.

The weekend, to Vicki's surprise, went well. The MP was not a bad lad, he was harmless and toed the party line. He knew what side of his bread to put the butter. He had the common touch and genuinely tried to help his constituents to have a better life, while furnishing his own little nest at the same time. Vicki thought he might make a good King. His wife was lovely, she was the most charming person Vicki had ever met. "I'm with you all the way Victoria," she said, "I saw your programme with the Yank the other night, bloody fantastic! Put that old Percy Greenhouse in the shade, mind you he could sort out my potting shed any day!"

The talk to the Regeneration people was a great success, although Vicki did not give too much away. After, at a party, Vicki meet some well connected people who might be useful to her. As she emerged onto the London streets, a car from the Sunday Billet, whisked her away to

Kings Cross and the train home. One thing that the newspaper had overlooked was that Liddingdale was on a branch line with no trains after the 19.50. Vicki gave Angela a call, "Can you pick me up?" she asked, "I need to talk to you, it's important." Angela was waiting at Leeds Central, she took her suitcase and steered her to a large police car on the forecourt.

"Sorry about this," said Angela, as she opened the door of the police car, "But I thought it might be easier to park, ok John, 17 Abbeyfield Drive please!"

"Can we go somewhere private?" asked Vicki, "I need to tell you something."

"Are you sure that you want to tell me something?" asked Angela in a policeman's voice.

"Yes," said Vicki, "Can we go to your place? I've been a bit naughty."

John dropped the two girls off at Angela's house. This was the first time that Vicki had been there. Angela made a pot of strong coffee and told Vicki to make herself at home. Vicki sank into a deep leather sofa and wondered if Peter had sat on it. Angela came back with the coffee and said brightly, "It's nice and strong, I find it helps people when they want to confess!"

Vicki's face went as white as it was ever likely to go. "I did it!" she said.

"Did what?" asked Angela with a broad grin.

"I blew up Abbey Wood!" said Vicki, "I'm guilty!"

"Of course you are," said Angela, "I knew that!"

"How did you know?" asked a startled Vicki.

"Because I'm good at my job, even I know that a gas leak is not going to make a hole that size, and what was

154

your new Dad doing in a caravan, with a woman, in November? apart from getting his leg over, bless him!"

"Are you going to arrest me now or later?" asked Vicki.

"Why ever would I want to arrest you?"

"Because I'm a criminal, I have to be punished, someone could have been killed!"

"But they weren't, and anyway it was a crime of passion, you'd get away with it, I would look silly. With millions of people behind you, I'd be trampled to death!"

The following week passed slowly, Vicki saw Jessie and Bill at the salon where she was told the wedding was on hold, because of problem with the Vendor's solicitor. Bill said he quite liked living in sin and it would be a strange God that would deny a couple of old people a bit of pleasure in their declining years.

Vicki hinted that she might be spending Christmas somewhere south of Syracuse in the company of an old bloke with funny glasses. "Go for it!" said Jessie. She then took Vicki to one side and gave her a hug. "I understand that I can't be your Mum," she said "But there is no reason on earth why you can't call me Aunty!"

"Is that what you want me to call you, Aunty Jess?" asked Vicki.

"Well it's better than my real name."

"What's that?"

"Gwendolen."

On the Saturday Vicki was booked to fly out to JFK in the evening. That morning she cleaned the house from top to bottom and buried the two gnomes in the garden. Her car was parked in the road, complete with suitcase. Around ten, the ambulance arrived, and she watched as

Peter was unloaded in his wheel chair. "Hello Darling," she said, "Pleased to see me?"

"Where were you going?" he slurred, his damaged body leaning dangerously forward.

"What do you mean?" asked Vicki.

"All dressed up and nowhere to go!"

"I'm off to New York!" she said.

"No," he stuttered, "You were NEVER GOING TO NEW YORK! You honestly thought I'd take you to New York with a face like that? ha ha ha ha!"

Vicki stared down on him, trying to look ugly, "I'm off, so goodbye!" she said.

"Even you would not leave me on the pavement, you love me, I'm going to get better, I'm going to screw your friend. I've got a lot of stuff on her and her superiors, so forget about New York!"

"Whatever you say dear," replied Vicki, and wheeled him swiftly down the front drive, making sure that the ambulance had gone. She rung the bell and Doris opened the door. "He's all yours!" she said, "He might last for a few years, probably die in his sleep, he's promised not to dribble!"

Vicki walked to her old car and drove away. At the airport she parked in the 'Short Stay Area'. She didn't bother getting a ticket, they couldn't charge her. After all, according to Liddingdale Police, the car didn't exist.

CHAPTER TWENTY FIVE

"SECOND THOUGHTS"

The second explosion at Abbey Wood had improved the town's fortunes. Ever since the rusty old crane had been blown to pieces, the town had prospered. All the publicity that had brought so much money into the place, had surprised Vicki. She just wanted the old crane out of the way so that she could have an empty bit of land for her park. It was a big area, much larger than Central Park. Over the Atlantic she had second thoughts about her 'Plan', she was worried that Gary would find a hundred reasons why it wouldn't work, and what was this professor like in the flesh? He certainly looked a bit odd.

Vicki's explosion on Bonfire Night had done the town a favour in a number of ways. Most residents were behind her idea for a wonderful park that would attract the world and his wife to Liddingdale, but if the problems with the landfill were insurmountable, at least for a time, people would still come to see the site of the 'Big Bang'. In the split second from when Bill pressed 'send', she had destroyed a corrupt and stupid Town Council, the biggest eyesore in the north of England, an unwanted development, and an ugly and unwanted megastore, thereby giving the local shops and economy a chance to thrive.

Vicki had never flown so far before and was finding the whole experience a little frightening. She closed her eyes and listened to that comforting drone all airliners make after a couple of hours. She found that it might be possible to sleep.

Somewhere to the east of Newfoundland, she drifted off, and for the first time in weeks did not dream of the Park. She was in the Market Place, there was a great crowd gathered but she didn't know why, then she saw that a statue was being unveiled. She pushed to the front of the crowd and saw that the statue was of her, complete with red face. She saw the inscription which read in large letters 'VICTORIA SMITH WHO SAVED THE TOWN'. There was nothing about building a park. On the ground was another statue that the new one had replaced, "Who is it?" she asked. She got closer and recognised her husband, Peter. "He killed the town!" said someone in the crowd. She woke up with a bump, the captain was starting to bring the plane down, dropping a few thousand feet and turning left over the Maritimes, heading south for Nantucket and Long Island.

Vicki thought about Peter. He didn't kill the town, nobody killed Liddingdale? The Romans building their road twenty miles to the east of the ancient cattle drove didn't help, nor did King Henry when he closed the Abbey. The downturn in the market for coloured glass and a big sandpit used for other people's trash was a major blow but the town had survived for a thousand years, it would survive another thousand. The plague, the dissolution, and two world wars had all taken their toll, it had limped its way through the lot! As the tyres slammed onto the tarmac and the brakes started to bite, Vicki was optimistic about the future of Liddingdale. She was not so sure if there was any future for Elysium.

Gary took the bus to Owego, he had never got around to driving. He had never got around to a lot of things. Gary's mother still lived in Owego, on the main highway. His late father had run a gas station and the remains of the old pumps were still there in what tried to be a front garden. The whole place, including the big house, was a little run down and untidy, like an old cat, asleep in the window of your favourite sweet shop.

His mother was pleased to see him, it had been some years since he had spent Christmas at home. Gary's Mum was in her eighties robust and sensible as a Ford pick up. When Gary told her that he might be bringing a lady from England with him, she was not impressed, "You have not been very lucky so far!" she said, "And that last one cleaned you out, I hope this is not serious!"

"This one's already married," said Gary, "Husband's disabled, we are not an item, she wants to build a park in England. There's a problem with the sub soil, I'm meeting her in New York City on Wednesday."

Gary's Mum prepared dinner in a large kitchen, straight out of Norman Rockwell. She made a huge meat pudding for Gary, who was well over six foot and weighed twenty stone. He was not disabled but walked with a shuffling gait. At school he excelled in the scientific subjects and loved the natural world in all of its forms but he was rarely asked to contribute to anything of a sporting nature. He was a trusting soul with a kindly disposition, but he had no idea about the real world, he liked it that way. After dinner he asked

159

his mother, "Are any of Dad's clothes still in the closet?"

"Yes there's some left, stuff that the church bazaar didn't want," said his Mum.

"Good," said Gary, "I need some new clothes for my trip to Manhattan, Vicki, that's the lady I'm meeting, wants me to look smart, like a filmstar!"

"There's that big old overcoat that your Dad used to put over the engine of the old Dodge Wreaker on Winter nights" said his Mum. "If you wear that, nobody will ever know what you've got on underneath."

At the airport Vicki saw a young man holding up a board with 'FAR NORTH TV' on it, his name was Winston he drove her in his yellow cab to a hotel in Lower Manhattan. It was early morning, there had been some rain overnight making the streets shiny.

Winston gave a running commentary as they drove along, Mannhattan starting to appear out of the fog. It was cold and damp. If this were a movie, it was an old black and white one. Two bridges were closed, so they took a detour, coming in through Harlem. "A TV company is paying for this cab ride," said Winston, "Are you famous lady?"

"No, not really, I'm just a little girl with a beat up face who's going to make the world nicer," said Vicki, trying to pick out the Chrysler Building and Empire State from a forest of spires."

"I'll say amen to that!" said Winston.

"Why aren't you driving a Checker?" asked Vicki.

"Lady," said Winston, "You're living in the 1975!"

CHAPTER TWENTY SIX

"58th STREET"

Vicki spent two days in New York before her date. She avoided Central Park and went south each day taking the bus and the subway. She had coffee in Greenwich, lunch in Soho and tea in Chelsea. New York was vibrant and exciting, even better than it appeared in the movies. The hotel was art deco, and her bathroom had trappings that any decent plumber in Liddingdale would have replaced years ago. She loved every bit of it.

Towards the end of the second afternoon Vicki took a ferry. At the Statue of Liberty the queue stretched back to the landing stage. She needed space and stayed on board. A man asked,

"Where are you bound for Miss?"

"Ellis Island," she replied.

"Next stop," said the man.

At Ellis Island the crowds were smaller, Vicki wondered around reading the names, trying to put faces to each one, faces of hope looking for a better way, a better life. She stood by the shore looking back to Manhattan.

When the rain came it was gentle. Since the fire the pain had never completely gone away and at first the rain made her face sting. Vicki started to cry as the raindrops and her tears blended, making patterns as they fell across her cheeks. At Abbey Wood the first snow of winter landed softly onto the black earth covering the deep wounds, nature knew best, she always would.

Vicki touched her cheeks, the pain had gone.

At Abbey Wood, the last flame died, the fire was out.

As Wednesday approached, a nagging feeling in the pit of her stomach, which had been there since JFK, started to infest the rest of her. In the early hours of the morning, she wondered what she was doing far from home, by herself in a New York bedroom. She studied 'The Plan' drawn carefully on good quality paper, perfectly folded and coloured in. What would Gary make of it? He was a scientist, top of his field, he knew all about rot and putrefaction, he was the top man. She was a housewife from a bleak northern town. She studied the 'Plan' over and over until drifting off each night towards a distant and unreachable Elysium.

Gary took a cab to Central Park. Gary the genius, who could not read a map or understand signs, was lost. After walking around in circles and asking the way a couple of times, a kind old woman took him to the Leob Boathouse and sat him down overlooking the lake.

"Stay there 'till your friend arrives," she said.

"Thanks so much," said Gary, "It's my first time you see."

"Say you like her hair," said the old woman, "Ladies like that."

Vicki left the hotel and walked the short distance to Broadway, where she turned and headed for Central Park. Vicki liked Broadway, it was different from all the other streets as it snaked its way to Union Square. It was flexible, it messed up the map, it didn't seem to care! The nearer she got to Central Park, the more apprehensive she became. At 58th Street she was there, all she had to do was cross an intersection. Central Park was staring her in the face across the street.

It was 10.55. She was against a wall, a wall of doubt, a wall of fear, a wall that was growing stronger and higher. Time was racing, people were racing, traffic was racing. She was drowning. With all her strength, she tried to call Gary. She got through at her third attempt, he sounded happy.

"Oh hi Funny Face!" he said, "I'm at the boathouse!"

"I'm so sorry Owego, I can't cross the road, I'm stuck at the 58th Street junction with Broadway."

"What's the time?"

"11.15, I've let you down, I'm so sorry, please come and get me."

"Of course," said Gary, "But I have a problem finding my way around, where's 58th Street."

"To the south, if you are facing the lake turn right, no, no left! I'll wait for you, I don't think I can move, please hurry!"

Gary did his best, but it took him over half an hour to find Vicki, shivering on a wind swept corner.

He gave her a big hug, her head reached the bottom of his chest. "What are we going to do now?" he asked.

They found a deli nearby and sat opposite each other at a polished table. Gary ordered fried eggs and coffee.

"I feel safe now, I'm ok now, I can cross the road, we can go back to the park," said Vicki.

"There's no rush, I understand." he said, "You've been through a lot, I've been doing my homework, tell me how you will build your Elysian fields, and then, you can take me back to the park, I'll never find it on my own!"

They both laughed, "Ok," said Vicki and put her hand into her coat pocket, but the plan was not there, she had left it at the hotel. Gary went to the counter and brought back some paper napkins and for the next thirty minutes they drew pictures and lines, circles and squares, much to the amusement of the owner, who kept them topped up with hot black coffee. Gary studied Vicki's plans, she could tell something was working inside his head. "It's a lot to think about!" he said at last, "Come on, let's go for a walk in the park!"

Vicki pulled him down the street, across the junction, and into the park, they meandered over to Strawberry Fields and on to Belvedere Castle, which Gary said was a contradiction in terms. Vicki said she had seen it in a movie, but couldn't remember which one. After walking around the Reservoir they stopped for refreshments at the Boathouse, where they should have started out. Gary had been very quiet and after a while, said, "When you have seen New York, will you spend Christmas with me? There's no commitment, it's not about you and me, it's about the Park, there's a lot to work out before we start digging."

"You think it might work then?" asked Vicki.

"Well yes and no," said Gary, he looked away, she grabbed his face, but he avoided eye contact.

"What's wrong with it?" she asked.

"Everything," said Gary, "I wanted to spare you, it's a nice idea though!"

Vicki felt as if she had been hit by a bus, "I knew deep

down I was wrong," she said, "But I so wanted to see New York, I so wanted it to work, I can't understand it, I thought you had been sent to help me."

"I was sent to help you," said Gary, "But I think you may have had some help before we met!"

"You know!" said Vicki with alarm, "You don't think that fire was accidental?"

"Oh the fire was natural enough," said Gary, "But that tower crane was pile driven into the ground with dockyard cables supporting it, a big gas explosion would have rocked it, maybe brought it down. That crane was blown to bits!"

"Are you going to turn me in?" asked Vicki.

"Course not!" exclaimed Gary, "You did what you had to do."

"So that's it then," said Vicki, "End of dream!"

"No," said Gary, "But first let me tell you why your scheme is not really practical."

They got up and walked slowly round the lake, Vicki put her arm in his, which made him walk even more lopsided. People didn't stare, this was New York.

"You wouldn't need to blow it up," said Gary, "That would be dangerous even for the Army. We don't really know what's down there. You could churn it up with a big machine, but there is a lot of it, and that would be dangerous for those working on site, let alone expensive. The chimney idea is ok, we already use something similar, but it needn't be that big and you would need more than one, we do need to draw off the gas, but that's not a problem we have the technology. Pushing it up to make a hill would be horrendous, remember, it's not just earth and stones, we have old car parts, glass, lumps of concrete, and plastic, lots of it! Once we get up to around twelve feet, we need a conveyor of some sort to build the cone.

Then there's stability, nobody could go near, it could swallow you up, a large part of the park, the centre, which is the focal point, would have to be fenced off!"

"Its hopeless then!" said Vicki, wishing she had stayed in the river.

"No, not hopeless, but I want to be truthful, and another thing," said Gary, "You can't have a glassworks there with an open flame."

"Have you finished?" asked Vicki, "Or is there more?"

"I think that's enough for now," said Gary, wishing he was better looking and a bit more tactful.

"That's it!" said Vicki, "It was a beautiful dream, but that was all."

"You can still do it," said Gary quietly, "We can still do it, but we must work with nature, she knows more than we do, when they made this park they had a clean sheet of paper and virgin land, we're dealing with a huge rubbish dump. Next year they have asked me to come over to England and have a good look at it, we just don't know what we are dealing with, but you've got the whole world on your side.

I've already told the authorities that I suspect there may be munitions buried up there, so you and your saboteurs are off the hook!"

"Thanks Owego," said Vicki, "Now tell me how to build my dream and I may marry you when my old man snuffs it!"

"Do you think we may get more money?" asked Gary.

"What do you mean?" asked Vicki.

"Far North Television!" said Gary, "They could make it a mini series!"

"It's a good job we are old," said Vicki, "Just think what the poor kids would look like!"

CHAPTER TWENTY SEVEN

"THE ANSWER"

They walked towards the Bethesda Fountain. A sun beam burst through a gap in the threatening clouds that were now starting to stack. The hum of distant traffic reminded Vicki of London. They were in an oasis of green. It seemed a slice of the city had been carefully cut out to reveal what was under its skin. Gary was silent, lost inside his head. When they reached the fountain Vicki pulled his great leaning frame down onto a bench. The sun went out, as it dropped behind the tower screen.

"What time is your bus?" she asked,

"Don't know," replied Gary speaking from a distant country.

"It'll be on your ticket," she said, "Look in your pocket."

"My ticket is at the bus station," said Gary, "In a locker."

"Why?" asked Vicki, "Did you think you might lose it?"

"Yes," said Gary, sounding like a child, "Along with my watch and credit card, I just brought a hundred dollars with me, I wanted to pay for everything. I wanted this date to be special, I'm not very good with people, the real world is a bit too much for me."

They sat watching the people go by, the day slowly started to die. Vicki stood up and said, "Can you find your way back to the bus station?"

"If I've missed the bus, can I stay with you? asked Gary, "I'm not really a city boy

"Of course you can," said Vicki, "On one condition."

"What's that," asked Gary with alarm.

"You tell me how to make it work, how to make Abbey Wood better, how to heal the wound."

"You may not like it Funny Face, and it's a long term solution, it will not be finished in our lifetime, but yes I know what to do, it's outrageous, but it will make you very famous and assure the future of Liddingdale, but it will cost. A few million for starters, that's of course if you like my idea, it's your dream remember, I'm just the kid from Owego."

Vicki pulled Gary into a semi-upright position, they shuffled up to the fountain,

"Try me," she said.

Gary took a deep breath, "Well first of all the land has been damaged, the earth has been raped, it could take thousands, even millions of years to heal." "Will it ever completely recover?" asked Vicki, dark shadows were starting to creep across the park which was melting into the night.

"Oh yes," said Gary, "Nature is a wonderful thing she will take back what was stolen, and when you come to think about it, it's all the same stuff."

"What stuff?" asked Vicki.

"We don't really know," said Gary, "I can give you all the technical jargon, but basically it comes from the stars. Stardust, that's what we are made of. One day, far into the future when our Sun starts to die, it will expand, swallow the Earth and take it back."

"Why do we treat every thing so badly?" asked Vicki, "Why are we so greedy?"

"Because we are flawed," said Gary, "It all goes back to the Garden of Eden, which is what you are trying to create down here on Planet Three. It's all there in Genesis, we were tempted and we know just a little more than we should, we want to play God."

"Do you think there is a God somewhere?" asked Vicki.

"I'm not sure," said Gary "But if there is, I hope it's a kind one, because all the troubles in the world, including Abbey Wood, are caused by us! Read Genesis, it means 'Origin' you don't have to be religious, it's all there in Genesis! Anyway, I'm starting to ramble, so let's get down to it.   First I would leave the landfill as it is, I wouldn't disturb it, some of the trash has been there for over a decade and has produced no problems so far, apart from the gas. As I've said before, we can deal with that. The main problems are twofold, how to grow things, and how to keep the people away and yet let them see it at the same time!"

"Impossible!" cried Vicki.

"Don't interrupt, I'll lose my flow," said Gary. He went to give her a playful tap on the head, his big clumsy hand missed and stroked her face, "I wish I could mend your face," he said.

Vicki stared wide eyed, pulled him down to her level, and kissed him, "It's time to go," she said.

"How far did I get?" asked Gary.

"You are going to leave the landfill to rot," said Vicki, more sharply than she meant to.

"Ah yes!" replied Gary, "Here's the clever part! We build two wide avenues, each as wide as Broadway, one north to south and the other across at right angles forming a cross. Now here's the answer and it's so simple! WE BUILD THEM ABOVE GROUND LEVEL LIKE TWO VERY LONG BRIDGES WITH A FANCY PALISADE ALONG EACH SIDE SO PEOPLE CAN LEAN OVER AND LOOK DOWN!"

"Let me get this right," said Vicki, as they left the park, "You want to build two very long bridges that cross in middle?"

"Yes that's right!" said Gary, striding off down the street, pushing commuters into the traffic, "And where they meet we will have a big circle, yes, we'll call it, now let me think…"

"The Circle?" asked Vicki.

"Yes that's it! We'll call it the Circle!"

Gary went quiet for a few blocks, then turned round and said, "Let's go back, I want to find that deli, we need paper, can you find it again? Let's eat!"

Vicki, who was hungry, steered Gary back towards the park, the street lights were now on, she thought she could find it in the maze. "What happens in the Circle?" she asked.

"In the Circle we build a tower, so that the people can climb to the top and see the whole park. Inside will be an Information Centre, we'll model that on the one in Central Park, as well as a shop and small theatre where we can get the message across!" Gary was on a roll, he continued, "The outside of the tower will be covered in glass, Liddingdale Glass, and there will be a needle on top, like the one in Dublin but it will be made of glass to reflect the sun." They reached the deli and went in, the owner recognised them and came across with a pile of paper napkins. He took two pens from his shirt pocket and asked, "You folks from out of town?"

"Up State," replied Vicki.

"Figures," he said.

Gary surveyed the menu, holding it close to his face.

"Where's your glasses," asked Vicki.

"What glasses?" said Gary.

"The ones that don't fit, the ones that your wore on TV!"

"Oh I borrowed those from a student," said Gary, "To make me look interesting!"

"So you don't need glasses?

"Well I have some but they are very old."

"Where are they?"

"In the locker at the bus station, by the way, do you like my new coat?"

Gary gave Vicki a couple of napkins and one of the pens, "There you are," he said, "Now you can draw the plan, remember one wide avenue top to bottom, one wide avenue side to side, big circle in the middle!"

"Haven't you forgotten something?" asked Vicki.

Gary looked at the table and said "Yes of course, the security fence, I don't like it but it will have to stay for a few years. My idea is to surround it with fast growing conifers, they will form a boundary to the park and protect it from high winds, we also have to fill in the hole that you made."

"Haven't you forgotten something else?" asked Vicki.

Gary looked at her and said, "Oh yes! The glassworks, we have to revive the glassmaking, I'm sure there is an industrial building or site somewhere near. It could have a visitor centre and a small museum, it should be free to visit of course, like the park, people are donating for this project. Only a politician would charge them twice!"

They ate in silence, both scribbling away on the paper napkins. Vicki noticed that she was doing most of the scribbling. After a meal that would have fed a small stadium, with a side salad the size of a house, Vicki said, "Gary this is the most wonderful day of my life together we are going to start something here."

She picked up her napkin, studied it carefully, held it up, and said,

"You are a genius, you are the smell of baking bread, a child walking for the first time, a weekend at Lake Louise, you are the circus coming to town, the Port Erin sunset, but Gary you've forgotten the most important bit!" And with tears streaming down her broken face, she handed it to Gary.

Gary looked at the small drawing, it was certainly neater than his own. Vicki had put in the avenues and the centre circle, an ensemble that looked like a flag for a new country.

"What's wrong?" asked Gary, "That's exactly what I have in mind!"

"There are no plants in the garden," said Vicki, "It's just a rough old landfill!"

"You are wrong," said Gary, "Into the Circle we will bring top soil, good stuff, and treat it with mulch, compost, and the like. We will grow flowers and shrubs in huge round containers, on the outsides of which there will be seats for the visitors to picnic on in summer. For the rest of it down below, we'll plant anything we can get our hands on. We'll see what will grow, trees, shrubs, flowers, anything and everything!"

"Will it work?" asked Vicki.

"Of course!" said Gary, who now had an audience of interested bystanders, "We'll lose a few, we'll find out what will thrive and plant more of them. The chemicals might kill off some plants, but we'll just put more in until the poison has gone! The plastic, and metal, and old bits of junk will help the trees to grip the sub soil with their roots, I know it's not the park you saw in your dream, we have to play with the cards we are given, and we haven't been dealt any aces."

Gary, who was now standing, looked down on Vicki, "What do you think?" he asked.

"Dreams do come true," said Vicki, "It's just that they turn out different than we expect." Gary sat down, took Vicki's napkin, picked up his pen and said, "There is one thing we haven't done, we haven't given it a name.

"ELYSIUM," said Vicki, "The land of the Gods."

Gary wrote on the napkin in his big uneven scrawl.

"What are you doing?" she asked.

"We have to name the avenues," said Gary. When he had finished, he handed the napkin back to Vicki and said, "How about that?"

She picked it up and read, by turning it round,

'AVENUE DES CHAMPS ELYSEES' & 'CENTRAL PARK DRIVE'.

"That's just perfect," said Vicki.

174

"And you know what?" said Gary, "I think we ought to call it 'VICTORIA'S PARK' after a little lady who had a big dream, after all you already have the Elysian Fields running across from one side to the other.

"Now show me yours!" demanded Vicki, "I want to see what you have drawn on your napkin."

"You don't need to," replied Gary, "You made a good job of it my effort's more an impression"

Vicki picked up Gary's napkin and was surprised when she saw that there was nothing resembling a park but instead he had drawn a picture of a little lady, "Who's this?" she asked.

"It's a beautiful princess that I met in Central Park today!" he replied.

"And did this princess have a funny face by any chance?" asked Vicki.

"I don't know," said Gary.

"You see I left my glasses at the bus station."